A HUSBAND IN WYOMING

BY
LYNNETTE KENT

MILLS &
BOON

Published in Great Britain 2015
by Mills & Boon, an imprint of Harlequin (UK) Limited,
Eton House, 18-24 Paradise Road, Richmond, Surrey, TW9 1SR

© 2015 Cheryl B. Bacon

ISBN: 978-0-263-25177-7

23-1015

"This should do it."

He placed the hat on her head, then turned her around to face the mirror above the dresser. "There you go. Looks good—you're already a bona fide cowgirl."

Jess gazed at their reflection, feeling the warmth of his body behind hers, the weight of his palms, his breath stirring her hair. Awareness dawned inside her.

"Thanks," she said, appalled at the quavery sound of her voice.

"Uh. . .you're welcome." Dylan sounded a little stunned, as well. He cleared his throat and stepped away.

This new Dylan Marshall—the grown-up version—was comfortable, satisfied. . .solid. His sexy grin, the confident and flirtatious attitude, the broad shoulders and narrow hips all combined into one seriously hot package.

But she would fly back to New York on Sunday, giving her only four days to get what she needed for the article.

But she was tempted to want more. Very tempted.

Lynnette Kent lives on a farm in southeastern North Carolina with her six horses and six dogs. When she isn't busy riding, driving or feeding animals, she loves to tend her gardens and read and write books.

Chapter One

June

Here comes trouble.

Standing outside the barn, Dylan Marshall watched as dust billowed up behind the vehicle approaching in the distance. He swallowed against the dread squeezing his throat. If he could have avoided this encounter by any reasonable means, he would have. The next four days were going to be absolute hell.

At last the Jeep came into full view, its dark blue paint now mottled with dirt. Going too fast, the car barreled up the last hill and hurtled along the road toward the ranch house, where it screeched to a stop with a spray of gravel.

Dylan shook his head. *Somebody needs to slow down.*

His boots felt as if they had lead in them, but he managed to move his feet and descend the hill toward the house. After a long day driving cattle, all he wanted was a shower. Dirt had settled in the bends of his elbows and the creases of his jeans, the cuffs of his gloves and at the base of his throat. He could taste it on his tongue.

He also wanted some dinner and a chance to sit down on a chair instead of a saddle. But most of all, he wanted to get clean.

He did not want to meet the press.

The door on the Jeep opened and a pair of high-heeled boots hit the ground. Standing up, the driver saw him coming, shut the car door and walked forward. Like two gunfighters, they moved slowly, warily toward each other, hands at their sides as if poised to draw a pistol and fire.

Dylan stopped with about ten feet between them. "Jess Granger?"

She was tall and slim, with long, shapely legs showcased by skinny jeans and those fashionable boots. Shiny brown hair whipped around her head, blown by the never-ending Wyoming wind.

Pulling the long strands out of the way, she nodded. "From *Renown Magazine*. You're Dylan Marshall?"

Her face could make Da Vinci weep—big eyes, the cheekbones of a goddess and a wide red mouth that stirred a man's blood to the boil.

He tipped his hat and then closed the distance between them, removing his gloves so he could shake her hand. "Welcome to the Circle M Ranch." A warm, slender palm returned his grasp. Dylan let go slowly, smiling in pure appreciation of her beauty.

Spreading her arms wide, she took a deep breath and blew it out. "There's a lot of space out here. Such a big sky."

"Are you a New York native?"

"I've lived there for half my life, so it feels like it. I've done my share of traveling, but this is my first time in Wyoming. I'm ready for a Western adventure."

"We'll do our best." A drop of sweat rolled down the nape of his neck. "Let me get your luggage." Stuffing his gloves into a back pocket, he crossed to the car and opened the rear hatch.

She whirled to follow him. "That's okay. I can—"

He pulled out her two bags before she could finish. "Got it. Come into the house." Leading the way onto the porch, he set down the big red suitcase and opened the screen door, nodding her through. "Be our guest."

He was determined to be polite. The only way to survive this interview was to keep control of the conversation, making sure Jess Granger learned only what he wanted her to. Reporters could be ruthless, but his job for the next four days was to give this New York journalist a peek at his life and his sculpture without actually revealing anything important. The gallery where he'd be showing his work had insisted on a big publicity push. Their bottom line: no article, no exhibit. After the way he'd sabotaged his career two years ago, Dylan knew he was lucky to get this chance for a significant show. If he wanted his work to be seen, he had to cooperate with the gallery—and with Jess Granger.

But he didn't want his emotional guts dissected in a fancy magazine for strangers to read. His three brothers deserved their privacy, as did the kids staying with them for the summer. Fortunately, Dylan considered himself an expert in the art of shooting the bull. Try as she might, he'd make sure Ms. Granger discovered only the most harmless details.

He set her bags by the hallway door while she sashayed inside and circled the living room. "Nice," she said, with a surprised expression. "Quite upscale for a bachelor pad."

"We try to stay civilized."

"So I notice." She homed in on the one sculpture in the room, a bear figure he'd made while still in high school. "Is this yours?"

And so it started. "Yep. An early piece."

"It's...clever. Obviously talented." Her words echoed the art critics he remembered from his time in that world—conceited and condescending. "But not at all similar to the work you were doing when you came out of college."

Hands in his front pockets, Dylan tried to stay relaxed. "I took a different direction for a while there, exploring new materials, new techniques. I tried to give people what they appreciated. What they wanted to see."

Jess Granger nodded, setting the bear in its place. "You certainly did that. For five years, you were the darling of the international art scene, the name everybody talked about. You had sculptures in the major art fairs and showed up at all the right parties.

"Then—" she turned around and snapped her fingers "—you disappeared. Just gone, without an explanation or a goodbye. There hasn't been a hint of news about you in more than two years. My editor was surprised to hear that you have a new show opening, and downright shocked that Trevor Galleries would sponsor this article."

Arms crossed, eyes narrowed, the reporter stared at him. "They sent me to get the story, Dylan. They want to read all about this comeback of yours. What does it mean, personally and artistically? What are your plans? Will you be returning to New York, or Miami? Or working in Europe? And, the most important detail... Why in the world did you drop out in the first place?"

Dylan cleared his throat. "You dive right in, don't you?" he asked. "Would you like something to drink or eat, first? A chance to get settled?"

"No. Thanks," she said, after a beat. "You had scholarships to European art schools. Blue ribbons at juried shows around the country. The critics all raved. You were a sensation before your twenty-fifth birthday. Why would you give that up?"

"Inspiration comes and goes," he said. "You can't always predict where it'll lead."

Jess Granger shook her head. "Artists don't just abandon their careers. What have you been doing in the two years since?"

"Working."

"On what?"

He shrugged a shoulder. "It's a ranch—there's a lot to do. In fact," he added, "I won't be able to sit around talking for four days. We've got a full schedule here in the summer, from sunup to sundown. Not including studio time."

"I'm not here to disrupt your life." Her hands went up in a gesture of surrender. "This article is supposed to provide positive press for you and your show. I intend to convey how you blend your art with your lifestyle."

"Sure. 'A Day on the Ranch' is all you want."

"I can't force you to confess." She actually pouted at him, making the most of that beautiful mouth.

Dylan only grinned at her. "With your looks, I suspect you can persuade a man to confide all his most dastardly secrets."

Her face eased into a sassy smile. "I promise not to reveal where you hid the bodies, anyway."

"I don't worry about that." Flirting was much more fun than dueling over the truth. "This is the Wild, Wild West, after all. It's the superhero tights in my dresser drawer I'm concerned about. We artists are a weird bunch, you know."

Jess Granger laughed out loud. "What a story angle!"

He enjoyed the sound of that laugh. "Anything to draw readers, right?"

"I do try to stay on the right side of the truth." Her sudden frown said he'd hit a sore spot. "So you'll have to show me the tights before I commit to print."

Dylan chuckled. "Once you're in my bedroom," he promised, "we'll see about that."

JESS WINKED AT HIM. "An interesting prospect." Maybe flirting was the way to get Dylan Marshall loosened up and talking. Otherwise, he'd stonewalled her so far.

And she certainly had no objection to trading banter with such a gorgeous specimen. He'd always been handsome, thanks to those long-lashed, dark chocolate eyes and a sensitive mouth framed by a square jaw and determined chin. Three years ago, though, he'd seemed too young to take seriously, wearing designer suits and an edgy haircut, dating top models and rich socialites. Observing from a distance, she'd considered him a brat. Talented, but spoiled.

Today, Jess had to admit that his exile had caused a huge change in Dylan Marshall, on the outside at least. There was a maturity in his face she found immensely appealing. With his narrow hips, long legs encased in snug jeans and broad shoulders under a blue-checked shirt, he could certainly lay claim to the legendary cowboy assets. He even wore a white hat, to finish off the hero image.

But her assignment was to get behind that image and discover the truth. Judging from his evasions so far, an aggressive approach did not bode well for the interview. She would have to handle him carefully, or she wouldn't get the details her editor demanded.

Before she could renew her offensive, a husky blonde dog padded into the room from the rear of the house followed by a big man with light brown hair and dark eyes like Dylan's.

"Welcome to the Circle M," the man said in a bass voice. "I'm Wyatt." He wore jeans and boots but had a back brace fitted over his chambray work shirt. "Make yourself at home."

Jess shook his hand, noticing calluses indicative of physical labor. "That seems pretty easy to do. I appreciate your hospitality."

"No trouble." He glanced at the canine standing beside him wagging her tail. "This is Honey. She runs the place."

"She's beautiful. Can I pet her?"

"She'll be insulted if you don't."

Bending over, Jess carefully stroked the tawny head. "Nice to meet you, Honey. You're a good dog, aren't you?" She didn't have much contact with animals, so she was never quite sure what to do with them. But Honey's brown eyes seemed friendly. Her tail wagged and she licked at Jess's wrist with her long red tongue.

"Wyatt's on restricted duty," Dylan explained as she straightened up. "He took a fall and broke a couple of bones in his spine. We're attempting to fill the gap he's left, but that's about as easy as trying to drive a truck with the engine missing."

"An exaggeration," Wyatt said, giving her a slow smile. "I understand you're from New York. Have you traveled much in the Western states, Jess?"

"I've visited Colorado and New Mexico for interviews, and I've skiied in the Rockies. But I've never had the chance to experience authentic ranch life."

"You're in the right place," Dylan said. "We're about as authentic as it gets when it comes to cowboys." He paused. "Well, unless you consider that Ford's a lawyer and Garrett's a preacher. They're a little out of the ordinary. Wyatt's the genuine article, though. A rancher through and through." He obviously admired his brothers and wasn't afraid to say so.

Footsteps sounded on the porch outside. "Hey, Dylan, get your butt out here. You're supposed to be—" Another cowboy in a white hat stomped into the house, but stopped short when he caught sight of Jess. "Oh…sorry. I didn't realize we had company."

"This is Jess Granger," Dylan said. "The reporter I mentioned would be here. Jess, meet my forgetful brother Garrett."

Garrett Marshall took off his hat and smiled as they shook hands. "I wasn't expecting you to arrive today. There's been a lot going on." As handsome as his brothers, he shared the same strong face and athletic build, but his eyes were blue, and his build was somewhere in between Wyatt's and Dylan's. He wore his light brown hair in a conservative cut and the uniform that ranch life apparently called for: jeans, boots and shirt. "I guess this means you won't be supervising the dinner detail," he told his younger brother.

"We've got seven teenagers staying on the ranch," Dylan explained when Jess glanced at him in question. "A sort of summer camp for some of the troubled kids in the area. My sister-in-law-to-be talked us into helping her out. So there's a bigger crowd than usual on the premises."

"That's quite a project." She didn't expect to be impressed with their efforts. In her experience, damaged kids couldn't be changed with a few weeks of attention, no matter how well-intentioned. "Sounds like a lot to fit in around ranch work *and* getting ready for an art show. When do you sleep?"

"Whenever he sits down," Wyatt said.

"Or stops moving," Garrett added.

Dylan rolled his eyes. "Thanks, guys. Just label me lazy in front of a reporter for a national magazine. No problem."

"We'll keep it off the record," she promised him. "What do the kids get to do while they're here?"

"Come observe for yourself," Garrett said. "They're not quite finished for the afternoon."

A distraction might ease Dylan's resistance. "Can I take pictures?"

"Sure, why not?"

"Let me get my camera."

"And a hat. That creamy New York complexion will burn in the Wyoming sunshine," Dylan said as he placed her bags in a cool, shadowed room off the hallway in the back of the house. "I hope you'll be comfortable in here."

The room had been furnished with rustic simplicity, soothing and peaceful, and the connecting bathroom was clean and bright. "I'm sure I will." She pulled her camera out of her shoulder bag. "But I didn't consider bringing a hat."

He nodded. "I figured you probably hadn't. Wait here just a second." The thud of boot heels retreated down the hall and then returned. Dylan appeared in the doorway with a white Western-style hat in his hands. "This should do it." Standing in front of her, he placed the hat on her head. Then he spun her around to face the mirror above the dresser. "There you go. Looks great—you're already a bona fide cowgirl."

Jess gazed at their reflection, feeling the warmth of his body behind hers, the weight of his palms, his breath stirring her hair. Awareness dawned inside her. She had to think about taking a breath.

"It's a new approach," she said, and was appalled at the quavery sound of her voice. "Thanks."

"Uh...you're welcome." Dylan sounded a little stunned, as well. He cleared his throat and stepped away. "You might want your hair in a ponytail—it's always windy on the ranch. I'll wait for you outside." In an instant, he was gone.

Releasing a big breath, Jess took off the hat and went to her suitcase for a brush and an elastic band. She took extra moments to thoroughly smooth and braid her hair, recovering her equilibrium in the process.

This new Dylan Marshall—the grown-up version—wasn't what she'd expected. She'd come prepared for a sulky, reclusive artist, someone hiding away from the world he'd once conquered.

The rumor at the time was, of course, that a love affair gone wrong had sent young Dylan into exile. No woman ever claimed to be the cause of his disappearance, though, and the attention of the art scene quickly shifted to a new talent.

The man she'd just met didn't appear to be pining away. He seemed comfortable, satisfied…solid. His sexy grin, the confident and flirtatious attitude, the broad shoulders and narrow hips—all combined into one seriously hot package. And there was chemistry between them. Those moments in front of the mirror had affected them both.

But she was flying back to New York on Sunday, giving her only four days to get what she needed for the article. With his three brothers as well as seven teenagers on the premises, there wouldn't an opportunity for her to get beyond a professional acquaintance with Dylan Marshall. Which was too bad, because she was tempted to want more. Very tempted.

But even if she had been staying longer, she'd reached the point in her life where a simple fling just wasn't enough. A few days…weeks…even months of good times and good sex didn't compensate for the emotional quagmire she went through when the relationship ended.

And it always ended.

Besides, her life was in New York. Her apartment and her job, her favorite coffee shop and the laundry that folded her shirts just right—all were in New York. Fun and games with the world's handsomest cowboy wasn't enough to make her give up her laundry service.

So she would keep her dealings with Dylan Marshall strictly business, and she'd leave with a well-written article and no regrets.

Above all, no regrets.

DYLAN FOUND HIMSELF out on the front porch without realizing quite how he got there. His brain had switched off, and all he could do was feel. Those seconds with Jess Granger's slender shoulders under his palms, her scent surrounding him and her eyes gazing through the mirror into his, had been...well, cataclysmic. He'd walked away a little disoriented.

Women didn't usually befuddle him like this, even beautiful ones. Ever since he'd discovered the difference between boys and girls, he'd made a point of getting to know as many of the opposite sex as possible—as friends, as lovers, as human beings. He considered women to be a separate species and thoroughly enjoyed all their unique, feminine attributes.

Somehow, he would have to maintain his usual detachment when it came to Jess Granger. He had to keep their relationship under control, avoid letting her get too close. She was, after all, a journalist. She'd come specifically to delve into his life and, more important, to reveal to the public as many of his secrets as she could discover.

Because of the person she expected him to be. The person he'd once been.

At eighteen, he'd left home determined to "make it big." He'd had talent but he'd also gotten lucky and done some sculpting that the "right" people thought they understood. They'd invited him to their playgrounds and he'd gone along because he was young and stupid and flattered by the attention. To a kid from tiny Bisons Creek, Wyoming, attending art parties in Paris, France, appeared to be the pinnacle of success.

He knew better now. His life in that world had come to a screeching halt one chilly afternoon during a conversation that lasted maybe five minutes. Later, standing in a Paris sculpture garden, he'd surveyed his own work and felt completely detached from its purpose, its meaning, its origin.

All he'd wanted at that moment was to go home. To be with his brothers, inside the family the four of them had built together. After years away, he'd craved the life he'd once worked so hard to escape.

He'd been on a plane less than twelve hours later. And once he got to Wyoming, he hadn't left in more than two years. He certainly hadn't courted the attention of anyone in the art world. But then Patricia Trevor called him, having seen a piece he'd donated to a Denver hospital charity auction. She suggested a gallery exhibit of his recent projects, and he was vain enough to say yes. He wanted exposure for his ideas as much as ever. If he didn't have something to say, he wouldn't spend time or effort on the process.

But he didn't expect his former fans to understand or appreciate this current approach. Jess Granger's article supposedly launching the show would probably bring down a hailstorm of derision on his head. That was the way the art world worked—you gave them what they wanted or they cut you off at the knees. In spite of her beauty—or maybe precisely because she was so beautiful—he expected the same treatment from her.

The screen door to the house opened and the lady herself stepped onto the porch, a high-tech camera hanging around her neck. "There you are." She squinted against the sun. "It is bright out here. Thanks for the hat."

"You're welcome." A compliment on how she looked in the hat came to mind, but he ignored the impulse. "Let's go watch the kids."

Walking side by side up the hill, Dylan found himself searching for something to say. "We took them to a rodeo and most of them decided they wanted to compete."

"Sounds dangerous."

"Not so far." They crested the hill and approached the group of kids gathered on the other side of the barn. "They're still at the learning stage." In the natural way of things, he would have put a hand on her shoulder to bring her closer to the action.

"Come watch," he said, keeping his hands at his sides and feeling as awkward as he probably sounded. "You can meet everybody. They're practicing on the bucking barrel."

The bucking barrel was a fifty-gallon drum suspended sideways by metal springs from four sturdy posts. With a rider sitting on the barrel, the contraption tended to bounce around, mimicking the motion of a bucking horse or bull. Ropes could be attached at various points, allowing spectators to increase the range of motion and the unpredictability of the ride.

"That's Thomas Gray Cloud." Dylan pointed to the boy currently riding the barrel. His dirty T-shirt testified to a fall or two already.

"All he holds on to is that one rope?" Jess shook her head. "I can't imagine. At least he wears a helmet."

"Ford, the legal eagle, made sure of that. But the secret is balance. You try to stay flexible and move with the animal, keeping your butt in place and using your arms and legs independently."

She looked over at him, her golden gaze intent on his. "Is this the voice of experience?"

He nodded. "I rode saddle broncs. The horses wear a special saddle—with stirrups—and you hold on to a rope attached to the horse's halter. It's slower than bareback riding, but style counts a lot more."

Her attention shifted to Thomas. "I think you're all crazy."

As they reached the group around the barrel, Thomas lost his balance and fell off to the side. He pounded a fist on the ground, but rolled over and got to his feet right away.

"My turn." A bulkier boy stepped up to the barrel. Thomas gave him a dirty look but backed out of the way, dusting his hands off on the seat of his jeans.

"Marcos Oxendine," Dylan told Jess. "One of our more challenging kids."

But today Marcos seemed to be on his best behavior. Grinning, he climbed onto the barrel, wrapped the rope around his gloved hand and yelled, "Let's go! Aiyee!"

The kids on the four corners began pulling their ropes, causing the barrel to tilt and sway in all different directions. Their encouraging shouts rang out in the afternoon air, recalling the roar of the grandstand crowd at a real rodeo. Marcos stayed on for nearly eight seconds, using his upper body to counter the motion of the drum he rode. When he finally did come off, he sat up laughing, while the spectators around him applauded.

"Again!" he demanded. "I'm doin' it again!"

Dylan glanced at the reporter beside him to gauge her reaction. What he noticed was that she stood with her hands in the back pockets of her jeans, and the stance did great things for her figure. He shifted his weight, cleared his throat and refocused his attention on the kids.

Marcos's second ride didn't last as long, but he moved away agreeably enough when Lena Smith marched up and announced that she wanted to go next.

Jess turned to Dylan with a shocked expression. "These events allow women to compete?"

"Yes, and there are a couple of women out there today riding against men. Lena is interested, so we wanted to give her a chance. And she's actually pretty good."

The girl proved his words, staying on for a full eight seconds, though Dylan suspected the rope pullers were going a little easy on her.

Still, she grinned when she got down. "That is so cool."

Beside Dylan, Jess Granger shook her head. "This was not what I pictured when you said you were conducting a summer camp. I thought, you know, arts and crafts—collages made with pinecones and sticks they pick up on a hike."

"Nope. We've been working on their riding skills—none of them could sit on a horse when they showed up here. On Friday we're taking them on their first cattle drive. You'll have to come along and observe."

"Um… I'm another one who's never been on a horse before I got here."

He gave her a wink. "We might have to work on that."

"By Friday?"

"There's a full moon tonight."

"That sounds like a threat."

"Could be. In the meantime, come meet my brother Ford and his fiancée."

Introductions took place as the kids dispersed, the boys heading to their bunkhouse and the three girls to the cabin they shared with Caroline. "They get an hour or so to reconnect with their phones," Caroline explained to Jess. "We wouldn't want anybody going into withdrawal."

"I certainly would, without mine. Dylan said that these are some of the troubled kids in your area."

"That's right. Most of them have had some kind of run-in with the legal system."

"They seem pretty cooperative, overall. Not as resistant as I would expect."

"Today's a successful day," Ford said. Caroline nodded. "And we've been together for a few weeks, developed some relationships. Do you have experience working with teenagers?"

"No, not really. But I have known some kids with problems." Jess Granger gave a short laugh. "In fact, I guess you could say I was one. I grew up bouncing in and out of the foster care system. At about the same rate my parents jumped in and out of jail."

Dylan swallowed hard, unsure of what to say. The Marshall brothers had lost both their parents before

Wyatt turned sixteen, but they'd always had each other to depend on. He didn't want to consider how hard life might be without some kind of family you could trust to take care of you.

After a few seconds of silence, Ford found the right words. "You've obviously not only survived that experience, but thrived."

Caroline put a hand on the journalist's arm. "I would love to have you talk to our kids, especially the girls. You're such a great example of what responsibility and persistence can accomplish. Please say you'll spend some time with them while you're here."

Jess Granger looked surprised. "If you think it will help, I'd be glad to."

"You have to be careful around Caroline." Ford put his arm around his fiancée and squeezed her shoulders. "If she can find a way to use you in one of her causes, she will. That's how the Circle M ended up hosting this camp in the first place."

"The world needs people who push for ways to help others," Jess said. "They're the ones who make a difference." She turned to Dylan, still speechless beside her. "Would this be a good opportunity for the two of us to talk? I was hoping to see your studio, get some insight into your new work process."

He had plenty of reservations about that plan, but no valid reason to refuse. "Sure." To Caroline and Ford, he said, "We'll catch up with you two at dinner."

Then, with a sense of dread, he headed toward the studio, leading the enemy directly into the heart of his most personal territory.

JESS CAUGHT UP with Dylan as he angled away from the ranch house, across a downhill stretch of grass toward what seemed to be another barn, though this building was gray, not red like the one at the top. "You haven't said anything."

His handsome face was hard to read. "I admire your achievements, against such odds. Were you close to your foster family?"

"Which one?" She wanted to push his buttons, shake his self-control. "I lived with five different couples. Ten brothers and sisters. Not all at once, of course."

"That sounds pretty tough." They reached the corner of the building but he continued past it, toward a stand of trees where the land flattened out. The grass was longer here and greener than on the hill, bending and swaying in the ever-present wind.

Jess stopped to take some pictures, and had to catch up with him again. "Where are we going?"

"To the creek."

"Why?"

"You wanted to understand my process."

They stepped under the shade of the trees and the temperature dropped about ten degrees. Jess removed her hat to let the breeze cool her head. "That feels so good."

Dylan nodded. "Part of the process."

He'd taken his hat off, too, letting the wind blow his wavy hair back from his face. There was a straight line across his forehead where the dirt from his morning's work had streaked his skin below his hat. It looked funny, yet also appealing, since it spoke of the physical effort he'd made. Jess was suddenly aware of his bare forearms, his flat stomach and tight rear end. Taking a deep breath, she pivoted away to study the scenery.

Trees and shrubs grew right up to the edge of the water. Along the edge of the stream, the trees were interspersed with rocks and boulders, some as big as cars. The creek bed itself was covered with smaller rocks and stones, which created a sparkling music as the water flowed over them.

"Beautiful," she said, snapping more photographs, moving around to get different angles and light levels. "Like visiting a national park somewhere, but it's all yours. No noisy, nosy tourists traipsing around to spoil it." She grinned at Dylan. "Unless you count me."

"You're definitely nosy. Not too noisy, so far." He gestured to the big, level rock he stood beside. "Come sit down."

"Okay." She sat on the rock and he joined her, leaving a space between them. Shadows from the leaves above danced across them, a flicker of gold and gray on their faces. "Now what?"

"Be still for a few minutes. Listen."

Being still wasn't Jess's habit. Most of the time when she was sitting down, her fingers were flying over the keyboard, typing an article or doing research on the internet. Now, with nothing to do, she had to grip her hands together to keep them off her camera— there were several terrific shots she could get from this position, including some close-ups of Dylan himself. Profiled against the trees, he radiated a calm control that was the essence of the cowboy ideal.

An essence very different from the frenetic artist he'd appeared to be three years ago. What had changed him? Or perhaps the question was, what had driven him in the first place? How did a boy who'd grown up in this setting, with the kind of values his brothers clearly considered important, end up in the limelight of the contemporary art scene? How would his work be different now? Was he ready to step back onto the international stage? Or did he have a different plan?

Would he answer her questions honestly, or leave her to draw her own conclusions? How well could she get to know him before she had to leave?

Dylan turned his head to look at her. "What do you think?"

"I think I'm dying to see your studio."

He glared at her with narrowed eyes. "Are you ever distracted?"

"Not if I want to keep my job."

"Does your job depend on my article?"

Jess shrugged. "I'm as useful to the magazine as my latest work. And there are lots of hungry writers out there hoping for a break. I'm the only support I've got, so staying employed is kind of a high priority."

After a long moment of stillness, Dylan sighed and got to his feet. "Well, then, Ms. Granger, I guess we'd better get down to business."

Chapter Two

The door to the barn was blue, in contrast to the weathered gray boards of the exterior, with a full panel of glass panes. Dylan walked inside, then faced Jess and held out an arm. "Be my guest."

Cool air greeted her as she stepped over the threshold. "Air-conditioning?"

"Wood stays more stable at a constant temperature."

The scent hit her all at once, a combination of varnish and glue and trees that cleared her sinuses. "It must make you drunk to spend time in here. That's a powerful room deodorizer."

He grinned. "I guess that's why the hours go by so fast when I'm working. I'm always a little high."

"So this used to be a regular barn?" The space was huge, open from wall to wall and clear to the ceiling, except for the supporting posts. A staircase in the corner led up to a railed loft stretching halfway across, where she could see a bed and a couple of chairs. "You sleep here, too?"

Dylan shrugged. "I remodeled over the years after we moved out here—with help from my brothers, of course. It's convenient not to walk out into a snowstorm in the middle of the night when I'm falling asleep." Then he hunched his shoulders again, and grimaced. "You know, I really would like to take a shower. Why don't you look around the place while I do that? Then we can talk some before dinner."

"Great." Jess watched him jog up the steps, then turned to survey the workshop around her. Tables of various sizes, most hand-built of unfinished boards, filled the space. Dylan's work area appeared to occupy the center of the room, where hand tools lay neatly arranged by size and use—saws, chisels, screwdrivers and other arcane devices she'd didn't recognize. Several surfaces held pieces of wood, also organized by size, from the smallest chips to branches four feet long. Some tables held sticks and limbs that had been sanded, stained and finished to a smooth shine. They were beautiful elements, but not the kind of material Dylan Marshall had utilized in his popular, critically approved sculptures.

What had he been up to?

For an answer, she moved to the tables lining the walls of the barn, which held figures of varying sizes—from a slender, twelve-inch form to a massive piece at least four feet square.

"Oh, my God," she said, in shock. "What in the world has he done?"

She recognized the animal she was staring at as a buffalo, about two feet long and not quite as tall. A collection of sticks and branches had been fitted together to create the figure, each curve and hollow of the body being defined by a curve or hollow in the wood. Every piece had been separately finished and polished to a deep sheen, allowing all the natural variations in color and grain to contribute to the texture of the image as a whole.

"Amazing."

She moved to the next sculpture, a fish twisting up out of a river. The scales of the fish's skin, the lines of the body and the base of splashing water had all been created with the same technique, fitting hundreds of tiny sticks together to produce a unified whole.

Jess ran a finger along the fish's spine. "Incredible detail."

On the next table there was a stalking wolf, almost half life-size, and a rabbit stretched out at a run, both executed with enormous visual talent and technical precision. Walking around the room, she appreciated the many hours Dylan had poured into these sculptures. That bear she'd seen in the living room at the house had been an early prediction of this full-blown talent. No doubt there would be many buyers for these beautiful works of art.

But… She covered her eyes with her shaking fingers.

The response of the art world Dylan had once conquered would be scathing. Cruel. Because of who he'd been and what he'd done, when the critics evaluated these pieces, they would laugh. Then attack.

And her article, the one Trevor Galleries had sponsored as a comeback announcement, would be the call to arms.

Jess dropped her hands to her sides and shook her head. "Artistic suicide."

Why would Patricia Trevor, the owner of the gallery, choose this kind of work to exhibit? Her showrooms were known for presenting avant-garde, cutting-edge art. Surely Dylan was aware of that. Why would he expose himself to ridicule this way?

From the loft above, she heard the shower cut off. He would be coming down soon, wanting to get her reaction to his pieces. Expecting her to appreciate his output of the past two years.

She needed some time to frame a response. Panicked, Jess ducked under the loft and headed for the shadows along the rear wall of the barn. One of the tables she passed held small clay figures, probably models he'd made as he planned the larger wooden pieces. The entire surface of another table was stacked high with books—anatomy manuals, collections of wildlife photographs, volumes on working with wood, finishes and stains.

The table in the corner under the stairs was illuminated by a large hanging light and covered with sheets of paper. These were his sketches, Jess realized as she came closer, three-dimensional drawings of animals in different poses, from different angles. Some of the studies she recognized from the sculptures she'd already viewed, but not all. He clearly had ideas for more work.

Footsteps sounded on the floor above her. "Be down in a couple of minutes," Dylan called. "Just making myself presentable."

"No problem," Jess said loudly. "Take your time." She'd inadvertently glanced up as she spoke, but as she brought her gaze down again, a picture on the wall behind the drawing table caught her attention. She hadn't noticed any other hanging art in the studio, so this one must be important.

The drawing was deceptively simple—a woman

with a baby in her lap. Looking from behind the
woman, over her shoulder, the viewer could see the very
young child with its feet tucked against the mother's
belly, its head resting on her knees and its tiny hands
curled around her two middle fingers.

It's a boy, Jess decided. Something about the baby's
face convinced her of that fact. The delicate lines and
shadings were so persuasive, so filled with emotion,
she felt as if she was indeed standing in that room,
visiting with mother and child. She could almost hear
the woman's voice, singing a nonsense song, and her
son's infant gurgle in response.

Suddenly, Dylan spoke from right behind her.
"What in the world are you doing back here?"

JESS GRANGER WHIRLED to face him, her mouth and eyes
wide with surprise. "I didn't hear you come down."

He hadn't expected her to get this far into the studio. No one but him came into this space. "I can be
sneaky. There's nothing important here in the dark
under the stairs."

"Except for this wonderful sketch." She nodded toward the frame on the wall. "Is it yours?"

"No." Dylan pulled together a bunch of the papers
spread over his drawing table and started to straighten
them. He shouldn't be such a slob, especially with
nosy reporters showing up to investigate.

She wouldn't let the subject drop. "It's not signed.
Did you know the artist? Have they done other work?"

How was he going to get out of this? "We're here
to talk about sculpture, right?"

"Right, but—" She gasped and then leaned over to
pick up one of the papers on the table. "What's this?"

He saw the sketch and swore silently. "Not much. Just an…idea I was playing with."

When he reached for the sheet, she held it away from him. "This is your brother. Wyatt, right?"

"At least you recognize him." He wasn't sure how to get the drawing away from her, short of wrestling her to the floor.

And now she was in full journalist mode. "Are you working on this as a sculpture?"

"Just considering it."

"You haven't started. Why not?"

"What did you think of the stuff that's done?" Dylan said desperately. "Isn't that what you're here to write about?"

"It is." She blew out a breath and put the sketch on the table. "But you won't want to talk about that, either." Stepping around him, she went toward the main part of the studio. Dylan followed, as prepared as he could be for what lay head.

"These are fantastic sculptures," she said, walking along the line of display tables to survey the various pieces. "Lovely representations of the wildlife you obviously value."

"But?"

"But, Dylan, this is nothing like the abstract work you were doing in college and afterward—the cerebral, confrontational pieces that got you noticed. You know as well as I do, the art that gets talked about isn't a reproduction of reality. Nobody on the international art scene will be interested in a statue of a buffalo."

Truth, with a vengeance. He shrugged. "That's not my problem. This is what I came home to do. I won't apologize for it."

"I wouldn't expect you to. The question is, what am *I* doing here? Any article I write about your new style is going to bring down catastrophe on your head." She paused for a moment. "And mine, for that matter. My editor will not appreciate a neat-and-tidy piece about a wildlife artist. It's just not what *Renown* readers expect."

"I can understand that." He stroked a hand over the head of a fox on the table near him. "So cancel the article." That would mean she had no reason to stay, of course. He didn't acknowledge the sense of loss that realization stirred inside him.

But Jess was shaking her head. "Magazine issues are planned long in advance. I've got a certain amount of space in this issue. I have to write an article. And after my last assignment...well, I need to turn in good copy."

"What happened?"

She gave a dismissive wave. "I showed up to interview the next country music legend and found him having an alcohol-fueled meltdown. Smashing guitars, punching walls, throwing furniture. I waited two days for him to sober up. But then all he wanted to do was get me into bed. My editor was not happy. I need to revive my career with this piece."

"No pressure there." Now he felt responsible to help her keep her job.

"Exactly. Anyway, Trevor Galleries paid for ad space because we were doing an article on you. It's a complicated relationship, advertising and content." She continued walking, examining his work.

"No," she said, finally, "you won't be coming back to the contemporary art scene. Not with these sculptures. I'm going to have to find some way to slant this, make it work for my editor. I'll have to find another hook." She stared at him with a worried frown. "Any ideas?"

From being the subject—victim—he'd become a coconspirator. "All I can do is talk about what I know." He couldn't believe he was giving her a reason to stay, offering to expose himself like this. "Try to explain the changes I've made, the reasons I focus on wildlife now." Not everything, of course. Some secrets weren't meant to be revealed. Ever.

She didn't seem to be convinced. "That might work. The 'soul of an artist' kind of thing. But you have to be honest and open with me. I can't turn in a bunch of clichés. Not if I plan to keep my job."

"Got it." He would be spilling his guts so Jess Granger could remain employed. That was not at all what he'd planned to do with this interview. There would have to be some kind of payback. "But I want something in exchange."

"And what would that be?"

"The same access. To you."

Her hazel gaze went wary. "You're not writing an article."

"If I have to drop my defenses, you should, too."

"I don't have any defenses."

"Right. No problems at all with the foster care issue." Her cheeks flushed. He stared at her until she looked away. "Deal?"

A long silence stretched between them. "Okay. Deal." She pulled in a deep breath. "So tell me something I can use. Something about your abstract work.

What were you thinking when you created those pieces?"

Dylan propped his hip on the corner of the table under the fox and drew a deep breath of his own. "Okay. My second semester in college, I took a sculpture class with Mark Thibault. You know him?"

"Sure. He's a well-respected critic in contemporary art. He introduced you to the scene. 'The biggest talent I've come across' was the quote, I believe."

"Yeah, well. Mark exaggerates. Anyway, he challenged me to explore abstraction. No figures, no representative stuff. If I submitted that kind of project, he promised to fail me for the semester."

"You cared about grades? Artists are usually rebels in that respect."

He chuckled. "I had three older brothers who were paying, in one way or another, for that class. I owed them good grades. So I worked my butt off for Mark, but he was never satisfied. He kept criticizing, rejecting, pushing me harder and harder. The deadline was approaching for the final project, and I still didn't have a passing grade."

Her hands went into her back pockets. "What happened?"

Dylan gazed up at the ceiling he and his brothers had insulated and paneled with finished boards. "I was sitting in the dorm with some friends, drinking beer out of cans. As guys do, we'd squash the cans when we emptied them and pile them on the table." He cleared his throat. "In my intoxicated state, I started studying the cans, the shapes of them after they'd been deformed. I chose three that seemed interesting and worked on sketches, playing with their relationships to each other. When I sobered up, I figured out how to make forms using rusted oil drums and a hammer, filled them with concrete and then ripped parts of the drums off."

Jess was grinning. "And Mark loved it."

"Oh, yeah. I did, too—it was great to work on a larger scale, to physically manipulate such harsh materials. I felt like I'd opened a door and found a wild new world."

"Did Mark learn the source of your inspiration?"

"After that sculpture won a blue ribbon, I confessed. He just said, 'Whatever works, son. Whatever works for you.'"

She gave another of those rich, deep laughs of hers. "And an art prodigy is born."

"There you go." He glanced at the window and saw with surprise how long the shadows from the trees had grown. "We're going to miss dinner if we don't head for the house."

"Dinner sounds terrific." She brought her hands out of her pockets, relaxing the pose that distracted him. "Something about all this fresh air makes me hungrier than usual."

"Wyoming affects people that way." He opened the door for her to walk through. "But afterward," he warned her as they walked up the hill, "it will be your turn to bare your soul."

WHEN SHE AND DYLAN entered the house, Jess saw all the Marshall brothers in the same room for the first time. Four handsome cowboys, cleaned up and smiling at her, was enough to set her heart to pounding.

She fanned her hot face with her hand. "Taken together, you guys are a little overwhelming." Dylan looked especially fine, something she'd been trying to ignore ever since he'd surprised her in the studio.

Cheeks flushed, every one of the brothers hooked his thumbs in his front pockets and gazed down at the floor. Jess chuckled. "There's definitely a family resemblance."

An expression of horror crossed Dylan's face. "Say it ain't so!"

Garrett snorted. "You should be so lucky."

"Caroline's supervising cleanup in the bunkhouse," Ford said, ignoring his brothers. "She'll be over when the kids are done."

A voice spoke up behind Jess. "Dinner's ready. You all should come sit down."

Hearing the unexpected voice, she pivoted to find a blonde woman standing in the doorway to the dining room. A curly-headed little girl peeked around her hip.

"Susannah and Amber Bradley are staying with us for a while," Dylan explained as they moved toward their seats. "And Susannah's making sure we're all going to have to buy a larger size in jeans."

Jess couldn't believe the table full of food, all for an ordinary evening meal. A steaming bowl of stew occupied the center of the feast, surrounded by dishes of mashed potatoes, rolls, green beans and a tossed salad. "I can see why. I'm sure it's all delicious."

Before she could pull out her chair, Dylan had done it for her. Garrett did the same for Susannah, after she'd gotten the little girl settled in a booster seat. Opening doors, pulling out chairs—compared with everyday manners in New York, all this chivalry would take some getting used to.

A sense of unreality stayed with Jess as she ate. When had she last sat at a family table? For Thanksgiving or Christmas, maybe, at the last foster home she'd lived in. Not in the middle of the week, though. And that foster mother hadn't been very skilled in the kitchen.

"I was right. This food is amazing," she said, taking another helping of stew. "It's a lucky thing I'll only be here a few days." She met Susannah's gaze across the table. "You're a wonderful cook. Or maybe I should say chef."

Susannah laughed. "Cook, definitely." Her crisp accent hinted at an East Coast upbringing. She wore her fair hair in a knot at the crown of her head, with wisps escaping to frame her face—a beautiful woman in a household of handsome single men. The possibilities for romance were certainly plentiful, but she must already be married.

"Does your husband work on the Circle M?" Jess asked, following that train of thought.

Susannah winced. An uncomfortable silence fell over the room, till Dylan stirred in his chair. "Susannah's husband is...trouble. She and her kids are here to stay safe."

She felt her cheeks heat up. "I'm so sorry. Being nosy is a job qualification. But I didn't mean to touch on a sore subject."

"Of course not." The other woman had recovered her control. "You couldn't possibly have known. Don't worry about it." She glanced around the table. "Can I get anyone more to drink? Do we need more food?"

Groans answered her and for a few minutes they all concentrated on their meals, which Jess figured was a polite way to allow her to save face. She was quite sure she'd never met a family so mannerly.

But then, the families she'd grown up with weren't always the most respectable members of society. Some of them had tried. Some…had not.

"Jess, you're from New York, is that right?" Garrett sat directly across from her. "You'll find it a lot less crowded out here."

She nodded. "Wyoming has the smallest population per square mile of any state, doesn't it? I'm not used to walking around without dodging other people."

"When the teenagers congregate, you can find yourself doing some dodging." Ford winked at her. His dark gold hair glinted under the light of the chandelier. "They take up a lot more room than you might expect. Especially now that they're more comfortable with the place."

"How long has your program been operating?" Surely that would be a safe topic, after the disaster she'd created with Susannah.

"This is the first year," he said. "And we're in week three. The first days were pretty rough—"

"Try 'impossible,'" Dylan said in a low voice.

Garrett glared at him. "We got through them. And things get better every day."

"Till the next disaster," Dylan nodded, as if he agreed. "You can bet there will be one."

Garrett started to respond, but Wyatt spoke first. "What about this cattle drive you're planning to take the kids on?" His deep voice broke up the tension. "Where do you intend to go?"

Jess couldn't follow the references to different fields and pastures and fence lines and gates, but the brothers evidently reached a consensus about the route they'd be following with kids and cows. Susannah and Amber would be driving to meet them on the way with lunch.

"Wyatt can ride with you to give you directions," Ford said. "Think that'll work, Boss?"

"Sure." His glance across the table seemed almost shy. "If Susannah doesn't mind."

She gave him a soft smile. "Of course not."

Jess raised her hand. "Can I ride in the truck, too? I'd hate to miss the excitement."

Dylan frowned at her. "Now, I was planning to teach you to ride directly after dinner. You should be ready to join us on horseback by Friday."

Ford grinned. "In case that doesn't work out, you're certainly welcome to a seat in the truck."

"Thank goodness," Jess said with relief, and earned a general laugh.

Susannah stirred in her chair. "I'm amazed at how well you all understand the land and its character. What a privilege, to take care of your own piece of the earth." She pushed her chair back and stood up. "I'll clear the dishes. Garrett, the ingredients for ice cream are ready."

Jess started to rise. "Let me help."

But Dylan put his fingers over hers on the table. "Not a chance. You relax." The skin-to-skin contact shocked them both, and they jerked their hands apart again. He cleared his throat and reached for her plate. "We've got minions to spare."

"Everybody should have minions," she said, and he smiled without meeting her eyes. Jess realized she was holding the hand he'd touched in her other palm, and quickly laced her fingers together, setting both hands on the table.

Caroline appeared in the doorway of the dining room. "The kids are ready for ice cream," she said. "More than ready." To Jess, she said, "Come outside and meet everybody. They're pretty mellow after dinner."

Outside, a group of boys was playing catch in the open space in front of the ranch house. Three girls sat on the floor of the front porch staring at their phones. "Lizzie Hanson, Becky Rush and Lena Smith," Caroline said, indicating which name belonged to whom. "Girls, this is Jess Granger. She's a journalist who's come to write an article about Mr. Dylan."

Lizzie, a slender blonde wearing far more makeup than necessary, looked up from her phone. "A journalist? You mean, a writer?"

Jess nodded. "Yes. I write articles for a magazine."

"Did you have to go to school for a long time to do that?"

"Four years of college."

The girl heaved a sigh. "That's a lot."

Redheaded Becky nudged Lizzie with an elbow. "You could do it. You like to write."

"Do you?" Jess sat in the nearby rocking chair. "What do you write?"

Lizzie shrugged one shoulder. "Just stuff. Things I make up."

"Well, that's the way to start. The more you write, the better you get at it." She caught Lena's gaze. "You were riding the bucking barrel this afternoon, weren't you? That's pretty impressive."

The girl shrugged. "It's fun. Women can do the same things men do."

"Absolutely." Jess grinned at Caroline when Lena's attention returned to her typing. "Are the teenagers churning the ice cream?"

"That's the plan."

"I've seen pictures," Jess confessed. "But I've never actually eaten homemade ice cream."

"That's okay," Becky told her, with a grin. "I never had any till I came here, either. But it's awesome."

"Thanks." Jess grinned back at the friendly girl. She really didn't seem to be the troublesome type.

Garrett had carried the ice-cream maker out to the area in front of the porch and was adding ice and salt to the bucket. "Okay, guys," he called. "I need some strong arms over here."

The boys sauntered toward the porch. "Not exactly a stampede," Jess commented. "Typical adolescents."

"They wouldn't want you to believe they were enthusiastic." Caroline smiled while shaking her head. "Cooperation is not cool."

"How well I remember." Jess caught Caroline's quick glance in her direction, but she didn't say anything else. She didn't want her memories to disrupt the peaceful evening.

Thomas, one of the boys she'd watched this afternoon, took the first shift on the ice-cream crank. Caroline introduced another boy, Justino, who gave her a solemn "Hi," before sitting down next to Lena. They immediately became completely absorbed in each other, locking gazes and murmuring a conversation for their ears alone.

Jess looked at Caroline with a raised eyebrow.

"They kept it a secret," Caroline said quietly, "until after they got here. Ford and I have been standing guard duty to be sure they stay where they're supposed to be after lights-out." She gave a mischievous grin. "That has its pluses and minuses."

Ford opened the screen door at that moment and came to stand beside Caroline. Although they didn't touch, the meeting of their gazes was as warm as a hug.

With an uncomfortable fluttering in her chest, Jess shifted her attention to the ice-cream process.

"It's getting hard," Marcos said.

"Let me," Thomas ordered. "You been doing it forever."

Marcos shook his head. "You started. I'm still doin' okay."

The other boy pushed at his shoulder. "Give somebody else a chance."

Marcos rounded on him, fists clenched.

Seeming to come from out of nowhere, Dylan stepped between them. "It's my turn, guys. Stand aside."

Both boys retreated as Dylan bent over the ice-cream churn. He grabbed the handle but groaned as he cranked it. "This *is* hard. Can't be too much longer till it's done."

Jess couldn't decide if he was faking it to make the boys feel better. He did continue to rotate the handle for a while. But he'd averted a fight. She had to admire his presence of mind.

Once the churn was open, he came across the porch to hand her one of the two bowls he carried. "Enjoy."

"Thanks." She sampled cautiously, discovering a rich, smooth treat that rivaled any vanilla ice cream she'd ever tasted. "Wow. You must have the magic touch."

"A great recipe helps." Dylan settled into the rocker beside hers. "Lots of eggs and sugar and cream. Susannah makes a mean custard."

"Mmm." Jess didn't want to confess she didn't understand what he meant.

"What's your favorite flavor?" he asked.

"At home by myself with a movie? Mint chocolate chip. For my birthday, I go to a shop in Brooklyn and order Earl Grey tea ice cream. How about you?"

"As far as I'm concerned, the more chocolate, the better. Dark chocolate with dark chocolate chunks and dark chocolate syrup. On a dark chocolate brownie."

Jess found herself watching as he licked his spoon clean. Swallowing hard, she shifted her gaze to the darkness beyond the reach of the porch light. "I believe I get the idea."

Most of the kids had settled down separately to eat their dessert, except for Justino and Lena, who sat hip to hip. Susannah Bradley had brought Amber outside to sit on the other side of the porch, where they were joined by a boy Jess hadn't seen this afternoon.

"That's her son, Nate," Dylan said, when she asked. "He's a natural horseman—has taken to riding like he was born in the saddle. Speaking of which…" He grinned at her. "Are you ready for your riding lesson? The moon's rising."

She decided to call his bluff. Standing up, she said, "Sure. Let's go."

"Great." If he was surprised, it didn't show. "I'll take our dishes inside."

In a moment, he reappeared. "Right this way, ma'am."

As they walked away from the house, she frowned at him. "Do I remind you of your mother?"

"I don't remember much about my mother. She died when I was six." His solemn expression revealed more than he probably realized. "Why?"

"You called me 'ma'am.'" Now she felt foolish. "I'm not that old."

"Sorry. It's just a habit—we tend to say it to women of any age out here." He sent her a smile. "I'll try to remember you're sensitive about that."

"I'm not sensitive."

Dylan gave a snort.

"Just accurate," she insisted. "I'm only thirty-five." Eight years older than he was, in fact, which was another reason to keep their relationship strictly platonic. Except her reactions to him weren't following that rule.

Jess decided to change the subject. This was supposed to be an interview, after all. "I understand both your parents passed away when you were all quite young."

He nodded without turning his head. "Wyatt was sixteen and I was eight when our dad died."

"You didn't have family to take you in?"

"Not that we knew of." He shrugged one shoulder. "We did okay by ourselves."

"Have you always lived on the Circle M?"

"Not in the beginning. Wyatt got a job with the owner, Henry MacPherson. We all eventually came here to live and work."

They reached the top of the hill and headed toward the barn. Dylan strode ahead to reach inside the big, open door, and light poured out into the evening.

Jess stepped through and then stopped in surprise. "I've never been in a working barn before. In fact, this is only the second barn I've ever entered in my life." A high-ceilinged aisle stretched along the side of the building, its beams and paneling aged to a rich, deep brown. She took a deep breath. "What is that sweet smell? Kind of grassy, only…more, somehow."

"Hay." Dylan pointed up to a loft filled with stacks of rectangular bundles. "About five hundred bales of grass hay."

"Ah. Bales. No wonder horses enjoy eating it. Must be delicious." Walking forward, she started down a cross-aisle with partially enclosed rooms on each side. The lower halves of the walls were built of boards, but the upper halves consisted of iron bars. The entrance to each room was a sliding door. "These are stalls where the horses stay?"

Dylan had followed her. "Yes, they're stalls, though we don't usually keep the horses in here unless they're hurt or sick. They prefer being out to roam around."

Along the rear of the barn were compartments with full walls and regular doors. "Feed room," her guide explained, showing her a space that resembled a kitchen, minus the oven and dishwasher. He opened another door. "Tack room—for saddles and bridles, horse equipment in general."

"Oh, wow." Rows of saddles lined one wall, with racks for bridles on another. Jess took a deep breath. "I love the scent of leather. Mixed with hay, it's a very evocative aroma." Sensuous, even. But she kept that impression to herself.

"The essence of a barn, as far as I'm concerned."

When they walked around the corner, they arrived

at the other end of the aisle from where they'd started. A double half door looked out into a large dirt area ringed by a wooden fence. "That's the corral," Dylan said. "The site of your riding lesson."

Jess leaned her arms on the top of the door, relaxing into the warm, breezy night. "Where's my horse?"

He joined her to gaze out into the darkness. "On the other side of the fence, in the pasture."

"And this full moon you talked about?" The indigo sky was dotted with more stars than she'd ever witnessed. "I'm not finding it."

Leaning over the top of the door, he pretended to search. "Yeah. That's a problem."

"I guess I'll settle for a barn tour instead of a riding lesson by moonlight." Facing into the barn again, she leaned against the door and surveyed the interior of the building. "It's beautiful. And so neat. No dust or dirt anywhere."

"Old Henry MacPherson was a bear about keeping the place tidy. Now it's second nature to all of us."

"He didn't have a family?"

"No kids, and his wife died in her fifties. We're lucky he took us on after our dad died."

"That must have been especially tough, since you'd already lost your mom."

"Wyatt kept us together. He's one determined cowboy." Dylan leaned sideways against the door, arms crossed over his chest, his gaze intent on her face. "But it sounds as if you were on your own. No brothers or sisters?"

Her whole body tensed. "Is this my interrogation?"

He frowned at her. "I was thinking of it as getting to know you."

Jess blew out a short breath. "No siblings by birth. Some of the families I stayed with had more than one kid."

"I guess it would be hard to get close to anyone if you weren't sure how long you'd be staying."

This was not something she *ever* talked about. "Yes."

"Was this in New York?"

"I grew up in Connecticut. Different towns, depending on who I was living with."

"Do you still enjoy snow?"

She couldn't help laughing at the question. "I do, as a matter of fact. It makes the world all fresh and clean, at least for a little while."

"Me, too." He was quiet for a moment. "So you went to college, got your degree and now you're a staff reporter for a glossy, upscale magazine."

Jess let herself relax again. "Pretty much, I suppose. If you skip all the unsuccessful rags I wrote for during the first eight years or so."

Dylan's brown gaze focused intently on her face. "Where did you get your drive to succeed? We had Wyatt—he was just born responsible, I guess, and he made sure the rest of us grew up that way. Now we're trying to give these camp kids a chance to understand how they can succeed in life. Who did that for you?"

"Nobody did that for me." The confession broke some kind of dam inside her. She gripped her hands together, trying for control. "Sometimes they made the effort, but I wasn't ready. Or I'd get kicked back to my mother, have to start taking care of her again. One couple didn't have time—six kids in a two-bedroom house make for a lot of work. One couple was only in it for the check. And I was never in the same school long enough to get a teacher on my side."

When Dylan started to speak, she held up a hand. "I raised myself, reading stories that showed me how kids are supposed to grow up. Judy Blume, Beverly Cleary, Ann Martin and Madeleine L'Engle—I guess you could say they raised me. I grew up to be a writer because they showed me how to live. Libraries were my true home."

Pushing away from the door, she stalked down the aisle toward the front of the barn.

"Jess, wait."

She stopped halfway but didn't turn around. "I never saw ice cream made at home. Till tonight." Shaking her head, she waved him away and stepped out into the night.

Chapter Three

Dylan let her get about halfway down the hill before he went after her. "Jess, hold up."

She didn't stop until he grasped her upper arm. By then they'd reached the front porch. Fortunately, the crowd had dispersed and there was no one to watch.

"Haven't you heard enough?" Her hoarse voice held tears. "What else do you want?"

"Just to make sure you're okay."

Her shoulders lifted on a deep breath. "Of course. More courtly manners from the Marshall brothers. 'Chivalry 'R Us.'"

"That's right." Under his palm, her arm was slender, but the muscle was strong. "Why don't we sit down for a few minutes?"

Without answering, she stepped up onto the porch. Dylan let her go, though he wasn't sure she would sit down until she actually did so. He dropped into the chair next to her and set his elbows on the arms. "You owe me one."

She sent him a sideways glance. "One what?"

"One probing question requiring a self-immolating answer."

That got a ghost of a laugh. "Oh, good. I'll give it some serious consideration."

"It's a golden opportunity."

"I'm sure. You were never very open with interviewers back then. Always the same flip answers."

"They didn't want to hear the truth."

"I would have."

"Maybe. And then you could have torpedoed my brilliant career."

"Instead, you did it yourself." The ensuing silence was filled with expectation.

Dylan understood he had only himself to blame for the direction the conversation had taken. But no matter how beautiful Jess Granger might be—and she was damn beautiful, with light from the house windows glinting on her hair and shining in her eyes—he wasn't about to tell her *everything*.

"Artists change direction all the time. I'd said all I wanted to with that approach."

She raised one eyebrow. "After five years? When you were only twenty-five?"

"I have a short attention span."

"Which is why you now build sculptural mosaics with small pieces of polished wood."

"There's this medicine…"

Jess slapped her hands on her knees and stood up. "I get it. You're not going to give me the truth about what happened to drive you away from abstract art." She walked to the front door. "Then I'll say goodnight. It's been a long day."

Dylan joined her at the door, putting his hand on the frame. "I bet it has. You've come two thousand miles from your world to mine." Through the screen, he saw that the living room was empty. "And I should do some work."

She gazed up at him, though not very far, because she was tall. "That would be interesting to watch." Then she put her hand up to hide a yawn. "But I was up at four. I'd probably fall asleep with my head on a table."

"You can save that for another night." That full, rosy mouth tempted him mightily. Was it as soft, as sweet, as responsive as he imagined? It would take just a light taste to find out.

Jess's hand landed flat against his chest. "You're not doing that, either. Good night."

Before he could react, she opened the screen door and walked inside, then disappeared into the shadows of the hallway. He heard a door shut firmly.

"Guess she told you."

Dylan jumped at the sound of Wyatt's voice. "What are you doing sneaking around?"

"Taking a walk. How's the interview going?"

"Rough. She wants more than I'm willing to say."

The Boss stepped onto the porch. "What have you got to hide?"

His brother was another person who didn't have to know everything. "I don't want you and Garrett and Ford pestered with the kind of attention an article in this magazine can generate."

"What kind is that?"

"Condescending, disparaging, disrespectful. Or, worse, you could start getting calls from women who want to hook up with a single cowboy who owns his own place. They might even arrive unannounced."

Wyatt grinned. "Could be a way for Garrett to find a wife."

"You, too, for that matter." An instantaneous frown greeted that suggestion. "Even more important, these kids shouldn't be advertised across the country as problems. That label would stick with them for the rest of their lives."

"Excellent point. So how are you planning to handle this situation?"

"We're working on an angle, Jess and I." Though he had a feeling that she hadn't given up her basic agenda any more than he had.

"What the hell does that mean?"

"I'm not sure." Dylan raked his fingers through his hair. "The work I've been doing the last two years is... different from what she expected, which is another problem. I guess it's up to me to figure out an explanation she can use that doesn't drag my guts out in the open for everyone to study."

"I can see how she'd be surprised—that oversize concrete-and-metal style you worked with in college doesn't mesh with the figures you're making now." The Boss tilted his head. "For the record, I like the new stuff better."

"I'm sure you do." Dylan put a hand on his brother's shoulder. "The *Renown* readers won't, but they'll recover. Meanwhile, if I'm going to make some progress tonight, I'd better begin."

Wyatt closed the screen door between them. "Hope you get some sleep."

"Me, too."

Once in the studio, though, he couldn't settle down. The latest piece waited—a mare and newborn foal he'd started building only a few days ago. He'd meant to avoid cuteness, intended to convey the perilous nature of birth in the wild—of life in general. A happy ending wasn't guaranteed. For animals or humans.

Dylan paced between the tables as his thoughts ricocheted around his skull, which was not at all conducive to creativity. On this kind of night, he often went down to the creek for a little while and let the water's silvery chuckle soothe his mind.

Or would he just spend those minutes mooning over Jess Granger?

"Damn it." He stalked to the rear of the studio, under the loft, and went to the drafting table. She would be in here sometime in the next day or two, so he might as well get this mess straightened up. No one was allowed to view his sketches. They were for his use alone.

But as he organized the papers—a stack for the ones he had sculpted, a stack for the ones he might get to, the trash can for failures—he came across the drawing of Wyatt that Jess had found. In a moment, another human figure surfaced from the pile—a woman with a baby in her lap. Dylan sat down in the chair and laid the two sheets on the surface in front of him. He should throw these away, too.

But if he did, he would only draw them again, as he had so often over the years, always determined that *this time* he would take the project all the way. *This time* he would create the sculptures that lived in his brain.

He never had. And he wasn't sure why...except that when he tried, he came up against a mental brick wall that stretched higher, wider and deeper than he could reach. What he wanted to create stood on the other side. And he couldn't get through.

With a sigh, Dylan stacked the two pages, folded them in half and dropped them in the trash. There was no point in beating himself up over what he couldn't produce. He had plenty to do over the next couple of months to get ready for the gallery show, and he was comfortable with the work that had to be done. Letting go of those images would free up more energy for the tasks at hand. Artistic and otherwise.

With the remaining sketches neatly slotted inside a file folder, Dylan made his way to the mare and foal and sat down, forcing himself for the first few minutes until the process started to flow—

A knock on the door jerked him around and he swore as he dropped the piece of wood he'd just glued. What had happened now? His brothers rarely bothered him at night except for an emergency.

Through the glass, though, he could see this was not a brother. He opened the door. "Jess? What are you doing here?"

Her hair was loose again, rippling around her shoulders and lifting with the wind. She wore a bulky blue sweater over a T-shirt and what appeared to be plaid flannel boxer shorts, with sneakers on her feet. Her legs, minus jeans and tall boots, were shapely and smooth. Gorgeous.

"I couldn't sleep." She'd taken off her makeup, revealing light freckles over her nose and cheeks. "I thought I would come watch you."

"Oh." He cleared his throat. "Okay. Come in." The last thing he needed when he was having trouble working was an audience. Especially *this* audience. "I was about to make some coffee. Join me?"

"Yes, please." She drifted along the display tables while he brewed two cups. "Heavy cream and two sugars, please."

"I like mine sweet, too." He brought her a mug. "Is your room not comfortable?"

"Oh, no, it's great. Flying just disrupts my internal clock."

"I remember. Eventually you stop being able to tell what time it should be." They were standing by a bighorn ram he'd finished a few months ago. "I haven't missed that, the last couple of years."

"You don't enjoy traveling?"

"I enjoy visiting new places. My preference would be staying somewhere for a month—or six—and really getting to know the people and the environment. I'm not into 'if it's Tuesday this must be Rome.'"

Jess eyed him over the rim of her cup. "Not just four days?"

"You won't know everything about this place in four days or four months or years." He didn't mean it as a challenge.

But she heard one. "I think you'll be surprised."

So they were adversaries again. Dylan didn't intend to argue with her about who would win. "Anyway, make yourself comfortable—not that there are many decent chairs to sit in around here. I'm going to get to work."

"Thanks. Just pretend I'm not here. I don't want to disturb your process."

Yeah, right. Dylan lost count of how many mistakes he made in the next hour as he tried to concentrate with Jess Granger in the room. She'd rolled his desk chair out from behind the staircase and over to where he was working. He couldn't argue that she'd picked the most comfortable seat available. The problem was the way she curled her body into its leather embrace, knees drawn up and ankles crossed, looking all warm and cozy. That blue sweater didn't reach much below the hem of the boxer shorts, so there was a long length of leg left to view, if he happened to glance over.

Which he did, too often. And each time he found Jess's gaze intent on his hands. She didn't say anything, but he was constantly aware of her presence.

Eventually, though, the spirit of the piece drew him in. Dylan found his focus, fingering through the collection of wood on the table for the next element, making adjustments, setting the fragment just right. He worked until his neck began to ache, until his back stiffened and his fingers fumbled, until his eyes burned.

"Enough," he said, capping the glue and pushing away from the table. "I give in."

A single glance at Jess revealed she'd surrendered before him. Arms folded, eyes closed, she'd slipped down in the chair to rest her cheek on the padded arm. She was deeply asleep.

In his studio. At 3:45 a.m. What was he supposed to do about it?

He *should* wake her, walk her to the house and send her to bed in the guest room while he returned here. And how painful would that be, for both of them? There was a reason he'd built the bedroom loft. All he wanted at this moment was to drop onto the bed and pass out.

He *could* leave her in the chair to sleep, even if she might not be able to straighten up for the next three days. That would teach her a lesson, though he was too tired to figure out about what.

Or...there was a king-size bed upstairs, a place to get some real rest without taking a predawn walk through damp grass.

Dylan rubbed his eyes and then put a hand on Jess's shoulder. "Hey, you. Bedtime."

Her eyes slowly opened to show him the bleary, confused expression of the very tired. "Huh?"

"Let's go." He took her hand and pulled.

She sat up with the coordination of a rag doll. "I don't understand." Her eyelids drooped.

"I'm tired. We're going to bed."

He'd carried her halfway up the steps before his last statement fully penetrated. Jess came awake, twisting in his arms. "No. We can't."

"Yes. We can." He took a tighter grip under her soft, bare knees and her arms, driving himself to the top of the staircase. Keeping hold, he walked over to the side of the bed and set her on her feet. "Crawl in."

"No." This protest was weaker. When he pulled down the covers, she gazed at the pillow with longing.

Dylan was about to collapse himself. Palms on her shoulders, he sat her down, slipped her sneakers off and tucked her feet under the sheet before pushing her backward. "Sleep."

Before he made it around to the other side, she had rolled onto her stomach and burrowed into the pillow.

He scowled at all those curls flowing across his dark blue sheets. "Make yourself at home."

Then he grabbed the blanket folded at the bottom

of the mattress and flung it over himself as he sat
down in the recliner by the window. He'd spent many
a night snoring at the television from this spot, and it
was usually only a matter of minutes until he called
the day done.

This was, however, the first time he'd ever done so
with a woman in his bed.

Somehow, his favorite chair just didn't feel so comfortable tonight.

OH. MY. GOD.

Jess didn't even have to sit up to realize where she
was. From where she lay on her side, she could see
the railing of the loft in Dylan's studio, as well as the
top of the staircase. In such a comfortable position,
she could be only one place.

His bed.

She couldn't recall how she got here. Her memory pretty much blanked out around two thirty, when
she'd checked her watch while Dylan pursued his meticulous work at the table. Another cup of coffee had
kept her awake for a little while but not, apparently,
long enough.

Not remembering how she got up here meant she
didn't remember what had happened *after* she got here.
She seemed to have her clothes on, which was reassur-
ing, if not conclusive. No one's arms were wrapped
around her. Or hers around them. Also comforting.

If she turned over, would she be staring into his
face? Gazing into those dark chocolate eyes with their
teasing glint? Was he under the same sheet—was the
warmth she savored the result of sharing a small, dark,
intimate space with him?

Jess didn't consider herself a coward. She'd lived in bad neighborhoods, attended schools where violence was a daily event, bruised her knuckles on other girls' jawbones. But the possibility of confronting Dylan Marshall on the other side of the bed seemed only slightly less risky than leaping over the loft rail to the floor below.

Then she realized she could swing her legs out of bed, stand up and at least be on her feet when she confronted him. Big improvement.

When she spun around, though, she found the worst of her fears unfounded. The other side of the giant bed lay undisturbed, the covers still pulled over most of the pillow. She'd slept alone.

Blowing out a relieved breath, she ignored the regret lurking in her mind. She reminded herself that spending the night—actually having sex—with the subject of her interview violated her standards of professional behavior. Of course, she'd never been tempted before, but that didn't matter. Rules were rules.

All she could see of Dylan, in fact, was a single sock-covered foot sticking out from underneath a blanket draped over what appeared to be a recliner facing the television. Talk about standards—he'd let her have the bed all by herself, even though there was plenty of room for two people to lie down and never touch. She didn't know many guys with that kind of personal code—these days, everyone seemed to be looking out for their own good at the expense of everyone else.

And why not? Who takes care of you if you don't?

Dylan would, the treacherous part of her whispered. She ignored it. She had to.

Carrying her shoes, Jess hurried quietly down the stairs, resisting the impulse to stop and make a cup of coffee. She glanced at her watch as she pulled on her sneakers and slipped out the blue door. Five fifteen. The sun had yet to rise into the sky, but there was plenty of light, a sort of golden glow that promised a beautiful day. Soft breezes rustled the tree leaves, and she could hear birds. Real birds, not just pigeons clucking on the sidewalk. Her sneakers and her ankles got damp as she brushed through the grass—when had she last experienced dew? How long since she'd walked on anything but a sidewalk?

Only when she stepped onto the porch of the house did she consider that the door might be locked. Then she'd be trapped outside, sitting in a rocking chair in her pajamas, until somebody inside woke up and emerged from the house—which was just one of the more embarrassing situations she could imagine. Especially if that person was Wyatt Marshall, the most intimidating of the four. She had a feeling he disapproved of her enough already.

But the knob turned easily in her hand. This wasn't Manhattan, after all. Who needed to lock up in the middle of nowhere?

Slipping into the living room, Jess gently closed the front door. There was a little squeak, but surely not enough to wake anyone. Most people slept with their bedroom door shut, right?

As she crossed to the hallway, the aroma of coffee permeated the air. The Marshalls must have their pot on a timer, so the brew would be prepared when they got up. She had one on her coffeemaker at home. Of course, she usually got up about eight...

"Good morning." Through the opening to the kitchen, she saw Garrett Marshall leaning against the counter. He gave her one of his handsome smiles and lifted his mug. "Coffee?"

"Um...thanks." Pulling her sweater around her, Jess sat on a stool at the breakfast bar. Now she regretted not having put clothes on before going to the studio last night.

"It's a glorious day." He brought milk and sugar to the bar. "Been out for a walk?"

She wanted to lie. Or just run away. "Not exactly." A sip of coffee fortified her resolve. "I couldn't sleep last night, so I went over to watch Dylan work."

Garrett paused in the act of drinking. He didn't move, his face didn't change—he just stared at her.

"I fell asleep in the chair. And didn't wake up until a few minutes ago."

"In the chair?"

"Um...no."

He nodded. "I'm guessing Dylan slept in his recliner."

"What makes you so sure?"

"He prefers his women conscious."

Jess sputtered her coffee through a laugh. "And you know this because...?"

"Because Dylan doesn't take advantage of people. Well..." Garrett chuckled. "He might be a little lazy when it comes to chores. You won't catch him making a meal. But he isn't deceptive. What he says or does is the truth."

"The whole truth?"

"Ah. That's different."

Might as well do some work, since the opportunity had presented itself. "Did you and your brothers follow his career, before he returned home?"

Forearms on the counter, Garrett palmed his coffee mug back and forth. "For the record? I did. Ford was in San Francisco building his law practice, so I'm not sure if he realized what was going on. Wyatt uses computers because they're fast at calculations, but anything he reads on the internet probably contains the word *cattle*."

"What did you think of Dylan's work? His life?"

"His abstract work wasn't anything I'd ever have associated with my little brother. And as far as I could tell, his life was pretty much what you'd expect from a kid given too much attention and not enough responsibility."

"Why did he come home?"

"Because he missed us?" He shook his head and took a sip of coffee. "Although that was part of it, something else happened. Something that shook him to the very foundation of his soul."

"But he hasn't shared what it was?"

"No. And I wouldn't get my hopes up, if I were you." His stern blue gaze focused on her face. "Dylan keeps his secrets. He seems easygoing, accessible. But underneath, he's got some solid shields. Nobody gets all the way inside."

She could see how much that bothered him. As a minister, he might wish his brother would confide in him on difficult issues.

But to her chagrin, before she could say anything,

Jess was ambushed by a huge yawn. She had to cover her mouth with both hands to hide it.

Grinning, Garrett straightened up. "The kids are usually ready to start their riding about nine o'clock, after breakfast and cleanup. It's not six yet. You could probably grab at least a couple hours' sleep before then. Susannah will be glad to make you something to eat when you're ready."

"That sounds wonderful." Her eyes watered with weariness. "I appreciate the coffee."

"I'm up early every morning. Join me whenever you like."

Jess shuffled to her room, closed the door and fell facedown on the bed with her feet hanging off the edge because she still had her sneakers on.

The next thing she heard was a knock on the door. "Still alive in there?"

Dylan's voice.

"Sure," Jess mumbled, and could barely hear herself. She cleared her throat and tried again. "Sure. I'll be out in a few."

"Great. There's a pair of boots in the kitchen with your name on it."

A fast shower got her blood moving and within fifteen minutes she had dressed and braided her hair. Makeup posed a dilemma—sunscreen moisturizer, of course, but did she require the full work-up for a day on the ranch? Or should she keep in mind that this was a professional assignment and prepare accordingly?

She settled for mascara and lipstick, though the face in the mirror seemed unfamiliar. "Nobody will notice," she assured herself. "This isn't Manhattan."

In the kitchen, Susannah slid a plate in front of

her as she sipped her second cup of coffee at the bar. "There's more if you want it." Her smile was as sunny as the morning pouring through the big windows. "Enjoy." She looked over at Amber, sitting next to Jess. "Finish your cereal, sweetie. Then we'll go outside."

The atmosphere in the kitchen was cozy as Jess attacked a cheese omelet with crispy bacon and the best biscuits she'd ever eaten anywhere. Susannah seemed constantly busy—cleaning counters, putting away some dishes, taking out others. Jess felt as if she'd stepped into a TV show, one of those family sitcoms from the sixties where the mother stayed home and took care of the kids while the dad went off to work and made lots of money to keep them all comfortable. Where everybody loved everybody else and disagreements were settled with words, not fists.

A world she'd never lived in and wasn't sure really existed…until now.

Pushing her empty plate away, Jess groaned. "I'll be going home ten pounds heavier on Sunday. The plane will probably crash from my weight."

Susannah laughed. "You'd be surprised how much you work off just walking around. And Dylan said you've got a riding lesson, so that's even more calories. Your boots are over by the door." She turned to her daughter. "Are you finished, Amber? Ready to go outside?"

"Yes! Yes!" The little girl started scrambling off the chair before her mother could get there. In her hurry, she unbalanced the high stool. "Mama!"

On reflex, Jess reached out to scoop Amber up before she hit the floor. "Phew," she said, cradling the warm body against hers. She'd never held a young child this close in her life. "Gotta be careful," she said, a little breathless.

Amber wriggled hard. "Down. Let me down."

Jess put her feet on the floor, making sure she was steady. "There you go."

"Good catch. Thanks." Susannah took her daughter's hand. "Outside for you. Gotta run off some energy."

Watching them walk hand in hand across the sun-streaked wooden floor, Jess was struck again by the sensation that she'd stumbled into a strange, incomprehensible new world. "*Alice in Wonderland*," she muttered, shaking her head. "I've fallen down the rabbit hole."

"What's that?" Dylan stood leaning against the frame of the dining room door. "Susannah said you were here."

He was so damn appealing, with that engaging grin and the twinkle in those dark eyes. He'd already been working this morning, and his sleeves had been rolled up to his elbows, revealing forearms tanned by the sun and sculpted by hard work. The open throat of his plaid shirt, his broad shoulders under slightly damp cloth, the slim jeans riding low on his narrow hips...

A bolt of lust drove straight through Jess's body. She squeezed her eyes shut for a second, clenching her fists against the force of it.

"You okay?" Dylan said, straightening up. "Maybe you need some more rest." He started toward her.

She held up a hand to ward him off. "I'm great. So what's up with these boots?"

"THIS IS CASH." Dylan led Jess to the horse standing by the corral fence. "As in, Johnny Cash."

She didn't stand too close. "A black horse. Naturally."

"Come stroke his neck. He's as quiet as can be." He saw her swallow hard before she took the step that would let her reach Cash's side. "You haven't been around animals much, I guess."

"No. Pets and foster kids don't always mix well." She ran her palm along Cash's sleek throat. "He's smooth. Warm." Her nose wrinkled. "And he smells funny."

"Horses have their own scent. It's not Chanel, but it's one of my favorites." Dylan leaned close to Cash's face and took a deep breath. "Mmm." The horse blinked but didn't move. "See—he's really calm." He took a brush from the bucket he held and handed it to Jess. "Why don't you give him a brushing?"

Raising a skeptical eyebrow, she gazed at the brush. "How is that done, exactly?"

She got the hang of the process quickly enough, once he showed her the short, outward flicks that worked best for getting rid of dirt. "I've cleaned his feet already, so you won't have to do that," Dylan told her.

Her big eyes widened. "You clean their feet?"

"Even with shoes, their soles are softer than you might think. We make sure there are no rocks stuck in there to bruise them, no sores or other injuries. Now we can go get the tack."

In the tack room, he pointed out Cash's gear. "I'll bring the bridle and blanket. You can carry the saddle," he said, teasing her a little bit.

"Right." Jess walked gamely to the rack he'd indicated, grabbed the horn and the back rim of the seat and pulled.

Luckily, he was standing right behind her when she staggered under twenty-five-plus pounds of leather. Her body pressed against his, and Dylan pulled in a deep breath even as he clamped his hands on her waist to keep her steady. "Whoa, there. I thought you'd tell me what I could do with that saddle."

She blew an irritated breath off her lower lip. "I should have. But it's your equipment I dropped. I guess you can deal with it." Stepping over the saddle, she walked to the door before looking back. "I'll be outside with Cash."

When he followed her into the corral—carrying the saddle under one arm, the bridle over his shoulder and the blanket in his other hand—she stood near the horse's head, touching his nose with her fingertips.

She glanced up as he arrived beside her. "So soft. And he doesn't bite." Her smile, when her gaze returned to Cash's face, was sweet and young. Without makeup, she seemed more approachable, easier to accept.

Like someone he might have gone to school with. Dated. Even married.

"He's a good boy." Dylan slung the saddle blanket onto the horse one-handed, straightened it out and then placed the saddle. "Cash turned twenty this spring."

"Is that old for a horse? They race three-year-olds in the Kentucky Derby, right?"

"Right." He bent to tighten the cinch. "I wouldn't race him across the ranch, though he'd probably go for me if I asked. But walking you around, he'll be great."

In another minute, he'd fastened the bridle straps and put the reins over the horse's neck. "Now, I can give you a leg up or you can pull yourself into the saddle. Which do you prefer?"

She glared at him. "After that trick in the tack room, I'll do it myself, thanks very much."

He stood at Cash's head, just in case. "Left foot in the left stirrup. We always mount from this side. One hand on the horn, one on the back edge. That's called the cantle."

"Right." Jess stood for a moment, considering, and then put her hands where he'd instructed. From past experience, Dylan expected a groan and a fumble as she tried to get her foot high enough to climb into the stirrup.

So his lower jaw dropped when she lifted her knee practically to her shoulder, easily slid her foot onto the tread and lightly pulled herself to stand on the left leg before swinging her right over and sitting down on the saddle.

"Like that?" She grinned down at him, obviously pleased with herself.

His turn to scowl. "You lied. You've done this before."

"No, I swear. But you didn't ask me about what other sports I might practice."

"Such as…"

"Karate."

"Ah. That makes you a dangerous person to know." No surprise there. Dylan pulled his hat a little lower. "Time to ride. Take up the reins. Squeeze your heels against his sides."

By the end of thirty minutes, Jess looked at home in the saddle, as if she'd been riding for years. Before an hour had passed, she and Cash were jogging both ways around the corral. In her white hat, long braided hair and skinny jeans, she definitely took the prize for the prettiest, not to mention sexiest, cowgirl he'd ever seen.

But she's not a cowgirl. She's a reporter. He was having trouble remembering that fact, and even more trouble not taking this morning at face value, as an experience shared between friends.

He shook his head. *Friends. Yeah, right.*

"Good job," he said as she finally came to a stop in front of him. "The kids will be jealous of your skill. Except for Nate. He's as talented as you are."

She stroked the side of Cash's neck. "Where are the kids? I forgot to ask."

"Trail riding, as a last prep before the cattle drive." To his own ears, he sounded terse. "You should get off now. Even if you're in great shape, you might be a little sore tomorrow. Come out of the stirrups on both sides. Then bend forward, bring your right leg over and slide to the ground."

She vaulted off with the grace of a gymnast. "That's pretty easy."

"You make it look that way." Dylan led Cash to the fence and exchanged his bridle for a halter before removing the saddle and blanket. "If you want to brush out the sweat where the blanket has been, I'll put this stuff away." He headed toward the barn without waiting for her agreement. His shoulder blades itched as if she was staring at him while he walked away.

When he got back, Cash gleamed like a fancy black car. "Nice." They walked the horse to the far end of the corral, where Dylan took off the halter and let him into the pasture. Right away, Cash kicked up his heels and raced across the field at full speed, tail flying high.

Dylan snorted a laugh as he closed the gate. "A two-year-old colt with a twenty-year-old's knees."

Jess stood beside him. "I'm glad you didn't show me that version of him before I rode. 'Cause I can assure you, it wouldn't have happened."

He didn't answer. Couldn't figure out what to say. His brain warred with his gut, churning him up inside. Smart and stupid, safe and crazy, were all mixed up.

"Oh, the hell with it," he growled. "Let's get this over with." He turned to face Jess Granger, cupped her face in his hands and tilted her chin up with his thumbs. Then he kissed her.

Chapter Four

As far as Jess could tell, this would not be over with anytime soon.

His mouth was firm against hers, but not harsh. Just...inexorable. She might have predicted this moment when she first saw him yesterday. And she agreed—they should satisfy their curiosity and then move on.

But there seemed to be no end to the ways their lips fit together, or to the variations of sensation they could create for each other. She circled her arms around his neck, and the closeness changed their contact, melding them more deeply. Their tongues touched, tangled, and they both gasped. His scent reached her—the tang of lemon, a trace of pine and an edge of spice, blended with the sweet musk of his sweat. The way her head spun, Jess could have been totally intoxicated at eleven o'clock in the morning.

Perhaps that was why she was so swept away, so overwhelmed and enthralled. Dylan's kisses confirmed a link between them, a spiritual connection she'd never thought she'd have. His solace and support, his concern and confidence, blanketed all the cold places inside her. She'd waited her whole life to get warm.

At the sound of a distant shout, though, Dylan raised his head. "Damn." His mouth looked as swollen, as ravaged, as hers felt. Staring into his face, she imagined his lashes might be wet.

"What's wrong?" She grabbed his biceps to keep herself upright. Her knees were too shaky to depend on.

"They're coming this way."

Jess followed his line of sight and saw a string of riders cresting the top of a distant hill. They hadn't reached the far pasture fence, but it wouldn't be too long.

His fingers untangled from her hair. He took a deep breath and stepped away, dropping his hands. "I've made a mess…there's a bathroom in the barn, with a mirror. You should go."

"Sure. Okay." She made her fingers loosen on his arms. "Yes."

"I believe the kids are expecting you for lunch," he said. "A picnic at the creek. But I've got some… chores to do, so I might not get there in time." After a pause, he added, "See you later."

Before she could say anything, he climbed the gate and dropped over to the other side. He walked to a beautiful white horse with brown spots all over its coat. They greeted each other with what Jess considered a hug—the animal folded its long head over Dylan's shoulder while his arms went around its neck.

The horse raised its head and in the next instant Dylan somehow threw himself up and onto its bare back, a maneuver that made mounting with a stirrup from the ground seem clumsy and silly. Without saddle or bridle, they started to move at a walk and then a jog, as she had with Cash, and then into a smooth motion that reminded her of a sailboat on a rolling sea. Although the kids on their horses were getting closer, Dylan rode off in a different direction, and then down a hill until he was lost from her sight.

Quite an exit.

Once within the cool shadows of the barn, Jess found the bathroom and locked herself inside. She sat on the small bench against the wall and pressed a wet towel over her face, striving for composure that was a long while coming.

They were just kisses. You're thirty-five years old. Not fifteen.

But no one had ever kissed her like that. No man had ever offered her such a spectrum of experiences— mental, physical, emotional—and touched only her face. Sex was sex and she'd had her share, most of it good, some of it terrific. None of it could compare with what had just taken place.

Or maybe that was simply what she wanted to feel, what she wanted to believe had happened. Dylan Marshall had gotten to her, somehow. For whatever reason, she needed this to be something special.

Which was ridiculous. She wasn't here for a relationship. She didn't want a relationship. What she needed and wanted was a story.

But how could she pursue the article, after this episode? Her objectivity about him had been completely destroyed. Anything she wrote would be biased by the emotional reaction he'd incited. And by his reaction to her.

Wait a minute.

Was that the point? Had those kisses been calculated to produce exactly that response? Could Dylan Marshall be devious enough to seduce her as a way of slanting her work? Did he believe she could be manipulated?

Jess pressed the wet towel harder against her eyes. She didn't want to accept that Dylan could be such a slick operator. He'd flirted with her, she'd flirted with him, and she thought they'd both understood it as a way of finding common ground. Fun, but basically harmless.

Those kisses had not been harmless. Would she ever forget that soaring sense of completion when his mouth softened on hers, the exquisite sense of being understood?

Noises outside the bathroom signaled that the kids had arrived. Wearily, Jess stood up and went to stare at the mirror over the sink. She'd smeared mascara all over her cheeks, and the only soap she had to wash with was a rough green bar. As for her hair…luckily, there was a comb in the medicine cabinet. That damage she could repair.

The damage to her ego, her spirit, her…heart? She wasn't so sure.

DYLAN SLOWED LEO to a jog when they got close to the creek, and then finally to a walk. When they moved under the trees, the horse put his head down and began to graze. Sliding off to the side, Dylan walked to his favorite boulder and sat. A minute later, he stretched all the way out and put his hat over his face. With luck, he'd fall asleep and not have to think. Surrounded by water and grass, Leo wouldn't wander off.

Unfortunately, Dylan's mind wouldn't wander, either, but returned with excruciating accuracy to his most recent mistake. A mistake he would live with for a long time to come.

Just a kiss, he'd decided. *Her lips, my lips, nothing special, let it go.*

Not in the least. First, there was the smoothness of her cheeks against his palms. Cool, too, even after an hour of riding. And those big hazel eyes, deep-set and intense. Registering surprise and then, in the next instant, desire.

Which was a big part of the problem. Her mouth had been warm, soft and ready. He'd lost his head with the first taste. After that, the only consideration had been making her feel good, letting her do the same for him. Pure pleasure in the giving and the taking. His body stirred just remembering it.

She wasn't supposed to turn him on. He didn't want to want her. Hell, he *couldn't* want her—what would be the point? Come Sunday, she'd be flying off to New York and he would stay in Wyoming. End of story.

Besides, she came from a world he'd deliberately rejected. The women he'd met in the contemporary art world were beautiful, like Jess. Many of them were smart, like her. Would he bring them home to meet Wyatt?

Not only no, but hell, no.

Jemima, Constance, Amabel, Olivia…lovely ladies, all of them, busy enjoying their wealthy, privileged lives. Dylan had enjoyed their privileged lives, too—his sculptures had given him access to their parties, their adventures, their friendship. More than friendship, in fact. Just casual connections, though, which none of them had taken seriously. He hadn't, either.

Underneath his hat, he blew out a long breath. This line of thought was one he avoided if at all possible— another reason to keep his distance from Jess Granger. She wanted to take him back to that point in time, to probe the mystery he'd deliberately created. She wanted to know about Noelle.

Swearing, Dylan sat up and jammed his hat on his head. Leo glanced over and gave a snort.

"My sentiments exactly," he told the Appaloosa. "I won't go there." Elbows on his knees, head down, he pulled at a tall blade of grass. "I can't."

Kissing Jess had been amazing. Disorienting, confusing and exhilarating. But he was twenty-seven years old. He'd shared kisses with…well, with enough women to understand how the game was played.

Get over it. Move on.

A sudden chill poured through him, from brain to belly. Maybe he didn't understand the game so well, after all. What if…what if Jess Granger had used those kisses to pursue her agenda? Sure, he'd started it, but her response could have been calculated to… *stimulate*, for want of a better word, his cooperation. Maybe she planned to seduce him into telling her the whole truth.

"Not gonna happen." He stood up and walked over to his horse, swung up onto Leo's back and urged him away from the creek. He did have chores to do, and brothers who would pester him until he'd finished.

Not to mention a reporter to deal with who ranked up there with Mata Hari in terms of technique. But now that he realized her intentions, he could counter her maneuvers with a few of his own.

They called it fighting fire with fire. And Dylan couldn't wait to feed the flames.

THE KIDS' PICNIC took place beside the creek, but farther away than the place Dylan had shown her yesterday. Jess was given a basket of paper plates and napkins to carry as she walked along with the crowd, going downhill from the red barn and away from the house. In the distance, the rolling plains of grass that created the ranch were framed by the blue-and-purple peaks of the Big Horn Mountains. Above all of it stretched the clearest sky she'd ever seen.

Caroline stepped up beside her. "How was your riding lesson?"

"Enjoyable, as far as I'm concerned." Till the end. Or, maybe, especially the end. "Cash made it easy for me."

"He's a great old pony. Ford told me that Cash is the first horse Wyatt trained when he came to work on the ranch."

"He must be very talented with this cowboy stuff."

"They all are. Dylan started at the youngest age, and he's by far the best rider. Did you watch him go off on Leo this morning? I grew up with horses, and I'm not nearly so comfortable riding bareback. And without a bridle, forget it."

"Are you from this area? One of the neighboring ranches?" Talking about Caroline would be a way to avoid talking—or thinking—about Dylan.

Of course, talking about Dylan was her job. The

reason she'd come and the reason she wished she could leave.

Caroline nodded in answer to her question. "But my dad and I aren't on speaking terms—he doesn't approve my line of work. Though I'm still close with my mom, the Marshalls are my family now."

Jess stared at her with raised brows. "Is this the Circle M Home for the Discarded and Difficult? That would include me, of course."

To her relief, Caroline laughed. "Could be. In fact, I was wondering if you would be able to talk with the kids after lunch, since we'll all be together and they should be reasonably settled. Not a huge formal speech or anything, just a conversation about how you set goals and achieved them, even with a challenging background."

"I'll be glad to." They arrived at the bottom of the hill, to find that Susannah had spread a checkered tablecloth over the wooden table where the kids were placing the various items they'd carried to the site— plates of sandwiches, bags of chips, a big bowl of fruit and another of salad. Thomas and Marcos had managed to cooperate long enough to transport a yellow cooler of water for drinking.

"This looks wonderful." Jess handed Susannah the paper products she'd carried. "What a great place for a picnic."

"Isn't it?" Susannah glanced around, finding Amber at the edge of the water with her brother, Nate, standing right beside her. "The more I see of the ranch, the more I love it. Wyatt is so lucky to live here. All of them are," she added, with a flush rising in her cheeks.

"Does the creek have a name?" Though shaded by

tall trees, the banks of the creek itself were covered with rocks and boulders, which made perfect lunch sites for the kids.

Garrett stepped up to the table. "It's a branch of Crazy Woman Creek."

Jess pretended to think hard. "Let me guess— named after a legend about a Native American woman whose tribe was killed by soldiers."

"Or a woman settler whose family was killed by warriors." Ford joined them and began to fill a plate. "Take your pick."

"How about…" Jess grinned. "How about an independent woman who bought her own land, built the house by herself and ran the ranch her way?"

Leaning against a nearby tree, sandwich in hand, Wyatt chuckled. "In the old days, they would have thought that was the craziest story of all."

"Of course," Caroline said. "They all knew a woman couldn't get along in this world without a man to take care of her." Smiling, she elbowed Ford in the ribs. He nudged her right back.

"It's the other way around," Wyatt said. "A man needs a woman to take care of him." When they all looked at him in surprise, his cheeks reddened. "Seems to me."

"Then it's a good thing you and I have Susannah," Garrett told him. "At least for now."

Wyatt's face went blank. "Guess so."

Jess noticed that Susannah was sitting with her kids on a nearby rock—close enough to hear the comments and have her cheeks turn bright red.

The easy conversation left Jess with a smile on her face as the kids gathered to clean up the table. She surveyed the area, trying to choose a suitable amphitheater to gather them for her "talk." Taking her place on a nearby rock, she nodded at Caroline to indicate she was ready to begin. In another minute, an audience of teenagers had circled in front of her.

Starting out, she met each one's gaze directly. "Good lunch, right?"

The kids responded with nods and a "yeah" or two, but the standard adolescent apathy was on display.

When she said, "Especially the brownies," more enthusiasm surfaced.

Jess would work with what she had. "So, the point of this meeting is for me to admit to you that I spent a lot of my life in the foster care system. I was five years old the first time I went into a foster home, and I left the last one when I graduated from high school."

Thomas stared up at her from under his brows. "How come?"

She took a deep breath. "My mom did drugs, but not much of anything else. We didn't always have a place to stay or food to eat. My dad sold drugs, but he disappeared a lot. They spent time in jail, and I would be placed with people who would take care of me. Then my parents would be released and regain custody. We seesawed like that till I was old enough to leave."

Lizzie raised her hand. "Doesn't it bother you to talk about it?"

"Should it?"

"Well…aren't you…doesn't it embarrass you when your parents are…?"

"Criminals? Yes. But it wasn't my fault." She gave them all another straight look. "That's one thing you must understand. Parents screw up. You can love them, but that won't make them suitable role models. You have to separate who you are from who they are."

Marcos was drawing pictures in the dirt. "Did you get hurt?"

"I was never abused. The people I stayed with weren't always lovey-dovey. But I got food and clothes and medicine when I was sick."

Thomas threw a small rock toward the creek. "So what's the big deal? Why should we bother listening to you? Doesn't sound so bad—you got places to go where nobody beat you up. They weren't drunk every night and making you do bad stuff." He jumped to his feet. "Why are you wasting our time?"

"Because you've all made some bad choices in your lives. And I've been in situations where those same options were offered to me."

"But you didn't make mistakes 'cause you're just too cool, huh?" Justino shrugged. "Too bad we can't all be cool like you."

Jess nodded. "I know. I'm sorry for you."

There was a shocked silence, before the rest of the kids—and the adults—saw her grin and realized she was joking. Laughter broke up the tension and Thomas, looking flushed and uncomfortable, sat down.

"I'm not too cool to make mistakes," Jess told them. "I smoked—cigarettes and weed. I've tried pills, booze and coke. I cheated on tests, stole from grocery stores and had fistfights with other girls. And one boy. I won."

The kids were staring at her with wide eyes. She didn't dare glance at the adults. "I did everything any of you has done." She noticed Lizzie's self-conscious flush.

"But guess what? I didn't continue that behavior. I didn't get hooked on drugs or alcohol—I'd spent my whole life watching my mom craving her next fix and doing whatever it took to pay for it. I watched one of my foster dads die from lung cancer. I got caught stealing and spent a night in jail with women just like my mom, and I knew I never wanted to do that again."

Another deep breath. "In my first foster home, I made a friend. Trini was two years older than me, but she was really nice to a scared little girl. We got to stay together for almost two years till my mom came to get me. But Trini and I swore to stay friends. BFFs, you call them today.

"And we did, till Trini turned sixteen. After that, I would call, but she never seemed to be around. And when we did talk, she was...different. Impatient. Then insulting. When she left her foster home, she didn't leave me a way to get in touch with her. I found out, when I went back to my mom, that she was a gang member's girlfriend. He beat her up whenever he felt like it. One day he hit her too hard and she died."

After a pause, she said, "That's why you're listening to me. Because I've already made the mistakes and I know what happens when you do. Because the nice people over there who started this camp really want each and every one of you to have a life—a whole entire eighty-years-long life, with someone to love you forever and kids and grandkids and a home you share with them all, a job you're proud of, a sense of self-worth and confidence and peace that comes with making good choices. All of that is possible for each one of you."

Thomas raised his hand. "Do you have all that?"

Jess met his gaze and uttered her only lie. "I do."

WHY DON'T I believe her?

Standing behind the other adults, Dylan had arrived in time to hear most of Jess's talk to the kids. Her frankness didn't surprise him—she seemed pretty comfortable with herself and what she'd been through.

"Not the kids and grandkids part," she said, grinning at the teens. "But I have a great job and a great life in New York."

He noticed that she didn't mention a husband or significant other...or even casual friends to share her days and nights. Maybe that's what made him doubt she was as successful in her personal life as she claimed—from the very first he'd had the impression of her as solitary. Jess struck him as a person who preferred to remain unattached. Self-sufficient.

But she didn't want the kids to know that.

Lizzie put up her hand. "If you did all those bad things, what made you change? Why didn't it get worse?"

Jess nodded. "Terrific question. One answer— books."

Marcos rolled his eyes. "You read books on making mistakes?"

"You can do that," she told him. Then she shrugged. "But who wants to?" That got her a laugh. "No, I read stories about other kids. Novels about girls who had really awesome lives, and whose biggest problems were the mean children they had to babysit. Or getting a boy to like them."

Justino sneered. "Talk about lame." Lena punched him in the arm.

"I read about boys who traveled through time and space to save the world. Girls can do that, too, though there weren't as many of those stories when I was a teenager as there are now. I read about growing up in the middle of a place like this." She stretched her arms wide. "But without running water or electricity, when you plowed the ground with horses or oxen to plant your crops and you drove to town in a wagon."

"I hate reading," Thomas said. "It's boring."

"I bet I could find you a book that's not boring. The thing is, books show you what's possible, from stories about what has truly happened to stories about something so crazy you can't begin to believe in the truth of it. Books distract you when you're bored. They comfort you when you're sad." Jess swallowed hard. "Losing Trini was hard. She was my only long-time friend, and I didn't know what to do without her in my life. The only way I could get through the hours without screaming was to read. Fortunately, I found a series of books about magic, strange creatures and fantasy countries. I buried myself in that world when I couldn't face the one I lived in. Otherwise... I might have started making some really bad choices of my own."

She let the silence lengthen while the kids considered. "That series inspired me to start writing on my own. First I continued those books—wrote about what happened after 'the end.' Then I created new characters and put them in the world that author created. I became immersed in my own writing, and that gave me a way out of the pain and anger I experienced over Trini." Once again, she locked gazes with each and every kid. "You guys could do the same thing."

That suggestion earned a loud chorus of denial, though Dylan noticed that Nate and Lizzie remained quiet.

"It's true," Jess insisted. "Every single one of you could write a readable story."

"Why bother?" Justino asked. "Somebody gonna pay me to waste my time?"

Jess held out her hands. "They pay me."

"You're ol…you're a grown-up."

"I got my first check for writing a magazine article when I was seventeen."

"What did you write about?" Lizzie, again.

"Trini. A national magazine held a contest to get published and I won."

"Was there a prize?" Marcos wanted to know.

"Five thousand dollars."

They all stared at her with their mouths open.

"Wow," Becky said at last. "That would be so cool."

Dylan managed to keep his jaw in place, but he was impressed. Jess was, apparently, a star in her own world.

Thomas recovered his control. "Yeah, right. I ain't got a computer to write stuff on. Even if I wanted to, and I don't."

"Pencil and paper work just fine. In fact…" Jess glanced at the adults. "We could probably find some paper on this great big ranch. A few pencils. You guys can try writing a story."

Marcos fell back onto the ground and covered his face with his arms. "No way."

"Think about this." She leaned forward, her face lit with enthusiasm. "You can travel anywhere in the universe. Not just this world, but any planet, star, moon, galaxy. What kind of place would you go to? That's all you have to do—describe where you would go and one thing you would do when you got there."

Still lying down, Marcos groaned. "Sooooo stupid."

"Reading and then writing were my way out," Jess told them. "Trini's story drew the attention of colleges, and a college degree gave me what I needed to make a career. I'm not saying that all of you will become professional writers because you started reading. What I am saying is that books contain ideas. And ideas can take you anywhere you want to go."

"I'm not doin' it," Thomas declared. He started to stand up, but a glance at the adults behind him quashed the idea.

"Who's going to read it?" Lizzie looked almost as excited as Jess.

Jess got to her feet. "That would be your choice. You can share what you write, or not. I happen to believe it's worth the effort just to sit down and try."

Caroline walked around to stand beside her. "I agree. It's pretty warm out, so we'll spend a cool hour at the bunkhouse, imagining where we'd go and what we'd do. Then you all can get some rodeo practice before dinner."

"I'd rather eat dirt," Justino muttered.

"That could be arranged," Dylan responded under

his breath. Wyatt, standing beside him, heard and frowned.

"Don't forget to take something up the hill with you," Caroline called as the kids began to disperse. "We can empty the water into the creek."

"I'll get that." Dylan picked up the canister and climbed over the rocks with it. When he turned around, the group had already crested the hill and was headed toward the barn.

All except Jess.

"Some resistance is to be expected," she said with a wry smile. "But this might not be my most brilliant idea ever."

He dropped down off the last boulder, near where she stood. "The point of our camp, as I understand it, is asking them to do what they've never done before and to consider what they want from the rest of their lives. It seems to me you covered both those objectives."

"Maybe. Or maybe I just gave them something to complain about."

"Something different to complain about, you mean. Thomas and Marcos are always whining about this or that."

"From the things they said, though, I gather they don't have easy lives. One story can't change everything. But it's a start." She joined him as he walked away from the creek. "It would really be great if we had books they could keep."

"The Marshall brothers did some reading as kids. We probably have books stashed in boxes in the attic."

"You might not want to give those away. And these kids would probably really appreciate *new* ones. How many of them have ever had a new book of their own? The first novel I ever bought is still sitting on my shelf." Jess blew a frustrated breath. "I could order titles online, but they wouldn't get here until at least Monday. And I'll be gone by then. Which is okay, because you've got plenty of help. But…" She shrugged. "It would be fun to watch them discover stories. The way I did."

"Then I guess this is your lucky day."

She gave him a sideways look. "Because you kissed me?"

He'd said it without recalling that part of the morning. "Of course." He flashed her a grin and winked. "But also because I happen to know someone who owns a bookstore."

She pretended to be surprised. "There's a bookstore in Wyoming?"

Dylan scowled at her. "Spoken like a true New Yorker. Not only is there a bookstore in Wyoming, there's one in Bisons Creek."

"Never heard of that place."

"It's the town closest to us—you didn't pass through on the way in, but it's about a five-minute drive from here."

"Well, then, I can go right now, and bring back the books before dinner." She gave him a big smile. "That's terrific."

They reached the barn and saw Caroline heading from the ranch house to the bunkhouse with a ream of paper in her arms and a bundle of pencils in her fist.

"Writing stories," she called. "What a great idea!"

"Is she always so cheerful?" Jess asked. "And so busy?"

"Definitely busy," Dylan confirmed. "Though when we thought Ford was returning to San Francisco to work, 'cheerful' did not apply to Caroline. But since he's come home and they got engaged, she's all smiles. Ford, too, which is kind of weird. He's always been the serious one."

A wistful expression drifted through Jess's hazel eyes. "Lucky for them." Then she shook her head. "How do I get to the bookstore?"

He cleared his throat. "One thing about this particular shop—it's not always open. The owner is a friend of mine, Kip Glazier. He rode bulls until an injury took him out of the sport. Now he has a tidy little horse ranch to take care of, but he decided the area needed a bookstore, so he set one up. Let's go down to the studio and I'll call him to ask if he can meet us there."

Jess frowned when Kip said he couldn't arrive till four. "So I guess the books have to wait till after dinner."

"The kids will be mellower then," he suggested, and she laughed at him.

"Sure."

"We will, too. After dinner," he said, in answer to her questioning stare. "Why don't we get cleaned up, meet Kip and then have supper in town? We have an excellent bookstore *and* a diner in Bisons Creek."

"A booming metropolis. But that sounds good. We can work on the article while we eat."

"Right." He hadn't thought that far ahead—hadn't thought at all, in fact, beyond the idea that as long as they were in town, they could have a meal that didn't include teenagers or his brothers. Thinking ahead did not appear to be one of his skills today.

Bringing her to the studio again, for instance. Jess was prowling the room, examining the sculptures. "The whole is definitely greater than the sum of the parts," she said, staring at the eagle.

Dylan went over to make coffee. "I'll take that as a compliment."

"Be my guest. But the same was true of your abstract work. The figures you produced came in groups, and it was the relationship between the members of the group that gave the whole ensemble meaning." She accepted the mug he offered. "So why did you stop? Why is this—" she used her arm to indicate the entire studio "—more valuable to you?"

Dylan retreated as far as the table behind him would allow. Taking a sip of coffee, he tried to construct a reason that would make sense and convince her to leave him alone.

"I don't know how you'll package this for your audience," he said. "You must be an excellent writer, though, to have won that prize when you were seventeen."

"I am good. But a talent for writing isn't all the business requires anymore."

"Beauty and talent ought to be enough."

"What is it I'm supposed to package?"

He gulped down more brew. "First, there were the materials. Concrete, plastic, iron, aluminum—hard, usually. Unyielding. From there, it's a step to uncomfortable. Then there's the size—I was working with forklifts to move the sculptures. The cost of transport could eat up most of a commission fee, if there was one. How about the environmental factors? When the world decides abstract art has gone out of fashion, what happens to those pieces? A landfill, where they never degrade? Or a jetty on the ocean, maybe, with other big lumps of concrete. Trash. I was basically creating pieces of trash, which people decided they liked until they changed their minds."

She tilted her head toward the eagle. "How is this different?"

"If we threw all of these sculptures out onto the prairie, they would eventually become part of the prairie again. The glues would dissolve, the finishes would degrade, the wood would fall prey to insects and weather and degenerate. Inside, they will last decades. Outside, these all revert to their original components."

Jess nodded. "The materials speak for themselves— wood you pick up off the ground, natural glues, stains and finishes. And the size, of course, is manageable."

"These sculptures can be moved by hand. They're scaled to be appreciated as parts of our lives, not to overwhelm with brute force. When I was twenty, brute force appealed to me. Then I grew up and realized I couldn't impose myself on others, on nature. That wasn't how I wanted to connect with the world."

He closed his eyes for a moment, trying to create a whole from these different parts. "I guess all this boils down to the idea that I don't want to create sculpture in opposition to the natural world. I want my work to be an extension of the world I live in. Make sense?"

"Sure." Passing in front of him, she walked her mug over to the coffeemaker and headed for the door.

"I'll be at the house when you're ready to go to the bookstore. That gives you a couple of hours."

With the door open, she looked over her shoulder to meet his eyes. "Maybe by then you'll have figured out what would be so damn terrible about simply telling me the truth."

Chapter Five

At four fifteen, Jess was sitting in the living room, chatting with Susannah and watching Amber play with her baby doll—carefully wrapping and unwrapping the blanket and pretending to rock her to sleep. The little girl lifted her head when the door opened. "Dylan!"

The doll dropped to the floor as she jumped up and ran to hug his knees. Grinning, Dylan picked her up and tossed her toward the ceiling. "How are you this afternoon, Miss Amber?"

"Fine." Caught securely by his steady hands, she settled in the crook of his arm. "Did you come to play with me?"

"I can play with you for a minute." He wore a maroon-checked shirt with the sleeves rolled up at the cuffs, black jeans and boots. His damp hair waved back from his face, exposing his striking bone structure. At that moment, he looked more artist than cowboy. "What shall we play?"

"Horsey!"

"We can do that." He carried her with him and sat down in one of the recliners by the fireplace. The little girl slid down to sit on the points of his knees. Holding her hands and bouncing his knees, he said, "Ride a little horsey into town, uphill, downhill and all around." On the last word he straightened his legs and she fell backward, hanging upside down from his grip.

"Again!"

Watching the two of them, Jess couldn't help smiling. Amber's giggles made her think of a bubble bath with froth you could hear. A glance at Susannah revealed a mother's love and pride, along with affection for the man entertaining her daughter. As for Dylan, he was enjoying himself, too. He would be a terrific dad one day, when he had kids of his own.

Jess sobered at the image that idea conjured up, though Dylan's future children had nothing to do with her.

Amber took four more rides before Dylan stood up and set the little girl on her feet. "That's your ride for the day, Sunshine. Ms. Jess and I have to drive into town." He looked at Susannah. "And we'll get dinner while we're there, so don't worry about us for tonight."

"Have fun," Susannah said as Jess stood.

Jess smiled at her, and walked through the screen door as Dylan held it open. By the time she stepped off the front porch, she allowed the smile to fade. She'd been angry when she left the studio two hours ago, and her mood hadn't changed.

Dylan came up beside her, his expression as stern as she'd seen it since her arrival. "This is my truck." He opened the passenger door of one of the big pickups parked near the house and shut it once she was seated. Climbing in on the driver's side, he started the engine, reversed the truck and then headed down the long drive she'd traveled yesterday, all without saying a word.

Jess had been driving yesterday, focused on her destination and not the scenery. Today she took a chance to enjoy the landscape—rolling green fields stretched to the horizon in every direction, with a backdrop of blue-green mountains and that incredibly blue sky arching overhead.

"This place is so beautiful," she said sincerely. "I love the flowers mingling with the grass." Blossoms in pink, yellow, blue and white popped up everywhere.

Without glancing her way, Dylan nodded. "Now you know my answer to at least one of your questions—who would want to work anywhere else?"

"I concede your point."

The remainder of the ride to town passed without conversation. Dylan didn't speak and Jess was certainly not going to venture another question for him to dance around.

Part of what he'd said to her this afternoon was probably true—environmental issues, the difficulties in creating gigantic art installations and the question of material use were debated in art circles year in and year out.

But she didn't believe those were his main reasons for deserting a promising career. Those were the kinds of concerns artists incorporated into their work, refining and evolving their style. No one vanished from view because he thought concrete was heavy and bad for the planet.

Dylan didn't *want* to tell her the truth. Pretty soon, she'd begin to suspect he'd murdered someone and run away so he wouldn't get caught. If she could discover anyone who'd gone missing besides Dylan Marshall, she might actually start looking for proof.

The little town of Bisons Creek fit into the cleft of two swells in the prairie, with a wide Main Street but no traffic light. Brick buildings lined the thoroughfare, their design more utilitarian than decorative, and the houses along the road tended to be practical instead of pretty. There were lots of trees, though, which surprised Jess. And many of the businesses had placed planters beside their front doors and filled them with brightly colored flowers.

"Is there a creek in Bisons Creek?" she asked. Watching, she saw the corner of Dylan's mouth twitch in what might have almost been a smile.

"Not anymore." He turned onto one of the streets that crossed the main road. "There was, when the place was settled in the 1890s. But highway construction diverted the water, so the town is now high and dry."

"Is that good or bad? I know there are lots of water issues in the West these days."

"In this case, it's a good thing. The creek ran along the east side of town. Old photographs show a muddy mess on Main Street when the banks overflowed. People are probably just as happy to live without that hassle."

Dylan stopped the truck in front of a small house with clapboard siding and a sign on the front porch rail that announced The Necessary Book.

"Cute name," she said as they followed the sidewalk to the house. "I hope he stocks at least seven readable books for teenagers."

"More like a hundred," Kip told her, when they

got inside. He was shorter than Dylan and whip thin, with dark hair and sparkling blue eyes. "Teenagers are my target audience—they're the ones we need to get hooked on reading and to continue. Come this way."

He led them into what would once have been a bedroom, but was now painted black with fluorescent designs scrawled on the walls in chalk. "Kinda crazy, but I get decorating advice from my teenaged nieces." Beanbag chairs in neon colors sat in the center of the room, with bookcases of various sizes and colors lining the walls. "I'm sure we can find what you're searching for in here."

"Pretty terrific, if you ask me." Dylan bent to examine the selection on one shelf. "If this store had existed when I was younger, I'd have been in here whenever we came to town."

Jess knelt by a different assortment to run a finger along the titles on the spines. "We need this one." She pulled it out. "And this, and this." Grinning, she looked up at Kip. "You're a treasure chest hidden in the middle of the desert. I may have to write an article about The Necessary Book."

Dylan gave a long whistle. "Better watch out, Kip. Give her an interview and she'll want to pry out your deepest, darkest secrets. Being a rodeo star, I expect you've got quite a few."

Laughing, Kip held up his hands. "Not me. Pure as the driven snow. I showed up, got on my bull, got off and moved on."

His friend stared at him, one eye squinted. "I seem to remember quite a few buckle bunnies clustered around that old jalopy of yours. Let's see, there was a Gretchen, and a Marla. Bobbie Jean and Terri…"

Walking on her knees, Jess moved to the next bookcase. "Not all secrets have to do with...um... romance." But it was interesting to note that his mind had jumped in that direction. Maybe those rumors about his disappearance being linked to a woman were truer than she'd realized. She would have to review her research and pull up the few facts she'd found. Having met the man, she might better understand what she'd learned.

"The best ones do," Dylan assured her, further piquing her interest.

At the end of an hour, the three of them had selected four times as many books as she'd intended to buy. "This way, they have choices," she said, handing Kip her credit card. "I can't begin to guess what each of them might select to read."

Dylan leaned an elbow on the counter. "I just hope they appreciate your effort. Your feelings won't be hurt if the reaction isn't exactly...enthusiastic, will they?"

Kip shook his head. "You are not the biggest fan of humanity, that's for sure. Our friend here used to be an optimist," he said to Jess, "always seeing the bright side. But since he came back home, he's taken a darker view, especially when it comes to the population of the planet. Some days, he's downright gloomy about it."

A glance at Dylan revealed that he was definitely gloomy about the direction of the conversation. "Reading the news these days is enough to depress Pollyanna. Have you got what you need, Jess? We haven't even checked out the rest of the store."

"I could spend hours just browsing." She picked up the bag of books. "But Kip probably wants to get home to his ranch. Thank you so much for opening up this afternoon." At the door, she looked back. "Can I call you about an interview? I'd like to run the idea of an article by my editor."

He shrugged. "Sure. I can use the publicity. Take it easy, Dylan. You two have a nice evening."

Jess frowned as she crossed the porch. Kip sounded as if she and Dylan were on a date.

The man in question stood at the bottom of the steps, hands held out. "Let me carry that for you."

"It's not heavy. They're all paperbacks." She stepped around him on the sidewalk and headed toward the truck. She couldn't decide what bothered her more—that this wasn't a date or that Kip had assumed it was one.

"Okay." Dylan got to the truck ahead of her and opened the door. "Let me hold the bag while you get in."

She glared at him. "Are women in Wyoming so helpless that their men have to do everything for them in case they hurt themselves?" She regretted the words as soon as she said them—there was no call for bad manners, even if she was irritated with...with somebody. About something.

But he took her seriously. "As a matter of fact, Wyoming women are strong, independent, capable and intelligent. And to show them how much we appreciate all they can do, we like to offer them special courtesies."

Jess expected him to turn around and leave her to shut her own door.

Instead, he simply took the bag away from her. "So if you'll climb in, I'll shut your door and then stow these books. Do you have a problem with that plan?"

What could she say? "No."

To his credit, he didn't slam the panel, but closed it gently. He did the same when he put the books in the back. By the time he'd seated himself and started the engine, Jess was feeling thoroughly ashamed of her temper tantrum.

"I apologize for being ungrateful," she said, staring straight ahead. "All this gallantry makes me nervous. I'm not used to it."

"I find it hard to believe that the men you go out with in New York don't use good manners."

"They aren't louts. They chew with their mouths closed." Not that she'd dated much in the past few years. Before she'd reached thirty, the Manhattan singles scene had lost its appeal. "Some of them open doors."

"Glad to hear it." He aimed the truck into the parking lot beside a building with a sign for Kate's Diner. "This is the best food in the county, except for Susannah's. Also the only restaurant in Bisons Creek." His grin emerged. "Shall I wait for you to come around and open my door? Would that restore your independence?"

"But then we might have to deal with your wounded masculine pride—a dangerous prospect. I'll let you get out on your own, thanks."

"You're sure?"

Jess scowled at him. "I'm hungry. Let's go find some food."

And some answers to her questions. She didn't want to provoke him in public, but an entire day had passed without any concrete progress on the interview. At this rate, she'd be making up the article as if it were a fiction short story.

As little as he wanted to cooperate, Dylan might prefer that solution, anyway.

DYLAN WASN'T SURPRISED to find the diner full of customers, practically all of whom he knew. He nodded and smiled at them as he guided Jess to the one open table along the wall.

"I'm going to pull out your chair," he said into her ear. A whiff of her cologne teased his senses. "But only because everybody is watching. Don't take it personally."

When he sat down across from her, she was smiling. "There does seem to be a lot of attention directed this way."

"That's a small town for you."

The smile faded. "I remember."

Before he could probe that reaction, their waitress arrived. "Hey, Dylan. Haven't seen you in quite a while. Guess you all are busy up there with those kids?"

"Hello, Ms. Caitlin. We are pretty busy this summer, with one job or another. This is Jess Granger, a magazine journalist. Jess, Caitlin's on the rodeo team at her college, planning to turn pro."

The pretty blonde nodded. "Barrel racing is my life. Are you writing about rodeo? I'd be glad to talk to you."

"Actually, I'm writing about Dylan, here. But I'm learning about rodeo, and I might be able to make an article on that subject work."

"You're writing about Dylan? That's cool. He was awesome with saddle broncs. I remember when I was a little girl watching him ride."

Dylan put his head in his hand. "Now I feel old. Just get us some drinks, Caitlin. Take your young self away."

"So old. You're all of twenty-seven." Jess was laughing at him. She looked so gorgeous, laughing… but then she sobered suddenly. "I've got as many years on you as you have on her. Now I'm depressed."

"Caitlin will be lucky if she's half as beautiful when she's your age."

Her eyes narrowed. "That doesn't help, thanks all the same."

He decided to challenge her. "Why not? You said this afternoon that you have a great life with all you could want. You wouldn't be able to say that if you were nineteen and just starting out."

"True. At nineteen I was working three jobs to pay for college, and sleeping four hours a night."

"What kind of jobs?"

"Waitress. Laundromat attendant—that's when I got my schoolwork done. Research assistant, where I learned how to mine the library and computers for information."

Caitlin brought their drinks—Dylan's usual iced tea and a diet soda for Jess. "The special tonight is fried chicken and gravy with potato salad, green beans and Kate's homemade rolls. Or I can bring you a menu."

"Do you have a big salad?" Jess asked. "Lots of vegetables? And vinaigrette dressing?"

"Sure. Do you want cheese or cold cuts on it?"

"No, thanks. But I would enjoy one of those rolls."

Dylan ordered the special and sent the waitress on her way. "You're the smart one, given how much

Susannah is feeding us. But I can never resist Kate's chicken."

"Ah, but I noticed all those pies in the cabinet behind the counter. I'm imagining the day will end well with a piece of coconut cream pie." She folded her arms on the table, elbows in her hands. "So let's get down to business here. Where do you envision your career going in the future? What is your long-range plan?"

At that moment, a hand landed on his shoulder. "Hi there, son. How are you doing?"

Dylan got to his feet to shake the portly man's hand. "Good, Mr. Harris. I hope you're well." He leaned down to kiss the cheek of the tiny woman just behind him. "Mrs. Harris, you look so pretty this evening. Did you get your hair fixed?"

She giggled. "You always notice, Dylan, dear. Wish somebody else would." Her gaze went to Jess. "It's so nice to see you out with a young lady for a change. I swear you live like a monk most of the time."

"The nicest girl in town is already taken," he said, but he felt his cheeks heat up. "This is Jess Granger. She's writing a magazine article."

"About Dylan? Well, that's very nice. Is this a magazine we can get here in town? We'll all be glad to read about our hometown boy."

"Um…" Jess obviously didn't know how to explain.

Dylan stepped in. "I'll make sure Kip orders a bunch of copies for his bookstore."

Mr. Harris saw Caitlin hovering at the end of the aisle with their plates. "We'd best let them eat, Merle," he told his wife. "Though this young lady could use more than just a salad, pretty as she is. Have a good night," he said, shaking Dylan's hand. "Don't do anything I wouldn't do."

"Which gives us a lot of leeway," Dylan said as he sat down. "I hear he was a wild one as a teenager. And if his grandsons are anything to go by, the stories are true."

"Oh, they're true." Caitlin set Jess's salad in front of her, and then gave Dylan a huge plate of chicken. "My granddad was one of his pals, and he tells some crazy tales." Hands on her hips, she surveyed the table. "Anything else I can get you right now?"

"A longer belt," Dylan suggested. "But we're fine, thanks." When Caitlin was gone, he looked across at Jess. "As we were saying before, I probably do know everyone in town. You said you understand what that's like."

"Did I?" She speared some lettuce and a cucumber slices with her fork.

"You mentioned growing up in small towns in Connecticut."

"I talk too much. But, yes, I grew up where people tend to know what you've been doing, where you're living, and can list the mistakes you've made. They remember you're a foster kid and they disparage you for that fact."

"Is that why you're living in New York City? You prefer the anonymity?"

"I went to NYU for college. And stayed for the jobs."

"You must have friends from school you still see."

"A few. But this is supposed to be my interview. Do you take your dates to other towns, so people here don't bother you?"

He sipped his tea. "They don't bother me. I'm always proud to be out with a beautiful woman for dinner."

Her exasperation was obvious. "This isn't a date."

"Is there a reason it couldn't be?"

"I'm here for an interview."

"Is there someone in New York who would mind that you'd gone out with me?"

"No!" She stared at him in frustration. "You're incorrigible."

"Just trying to get the facts." So she didn't have a lover or husband. At least he'd gotten one piece of information out of her.

"Without answering *my* questions."

"You're more interesting."

"*You* are the subject of the interview, damn it."

The entire restaurant heard her, and a short silence fell. Then conversation and clatter picked up again. Jess sat across from him, still glaring, her cheeks flushed red.

"Everything okay back here?" Kate herself stepped up to the table. A tall, well-built woman, she'd run the restaurant since the husband who'd named it for her had died ten years ago.

Dylan introduced her to Jess. "She's frustrated with me."

Kate nodded. "That's a pretty standard condition for most of us at one time or another. Dylan has his own ways of meeting expectations."

Jess nodded. "So I gather. I'm considering thumbscrews. Or the rack."

"His brothers probably have a few torture devices they'd allow you to use."

"I am not a problem," Dylan protested. "Ask me anything you want." He was taking a risk, but he figured he could handle the worst.

The reporter didn't say anything for a few moments, but eyed him with speculation in her golden gaze. "Why did you choose sculpture as your means of artistic expression?"

"I like being able to consider an object from all different angles. A subject changes, depending on your perspective."

"Slippery as an eel," Kate said, and returned to her kitchen.

But Jess seemed satisfied. "How do you decide what subject you want to work on?"

"As you saw, I make sketches of what I observe as I'm out working on the ranch. When I'm ready to start something new, I'll be drawn to one of those when I look them over. Or I'll witness a scene that stirs me, and go with that. It's kind of a random process."

"Do you build more than one sculpture at once?"

As long as she asked such specific, process-oriented questions, Dylan didn't mind answering. They talked until their plates were empty, until they'd each polished off a slice of coconut cream pie and a cup of coffee. The shadows outside had lengthened by the time Jess relaxed against the back of her chair.

"I'm impressed," she said, pulling her hair behind her shoulders. "No evasion or equivocation."

"You were throwing softballs," he told her. "Not even fast-pitch."

Her grin acknowledged that fact. "I wondered if Kate was going to have to play umpire."

"She would, if necessary. And she'd be good at it. Shall we head home to the Circle M?"

Jess nodded and picked up her purse. Dylan meant to pull out her chair as she stood, if only to annoy her, but Cindi and Dan Bowman passed their table just then, requiring an introduction and some chitchat.

Once the couple moved on, Jess got to her feet. "Beat you to it," she said as she walked by. Then she waved the check Caitlin had written up in front of him. "And I'm paying."

Short of wrestling over the piece of paper—which had its own appeal—there wasn't much he could do about the situation. "Apparently I'm not the only one who's sneaky," he said, holding the door for her to leave the diner.

"A job qualification for journalists," she told him as they walked to the truck. "You find out what you need to know by whatever means necessary."

"Is that a threat?"

"More of a promise. Or you could just tell me the truth and get the process over with. Like pulling a tooth—one quick jerk and it's done."

Dylan grinned at her as he started the engine. "Ah, but sometimes it's more fun to extend the process, make it last as long as possible."

She frowned and shook her head at him. "Incorrigible."

The sun hovered above the Big Horns as they drove to the ranch. Dylan rubbed his burning eyes a couple of times during the trip. The long stretch of working late was catching up with him, and he was going to have to get a good night's sleep pretty soon to keep him going. With luck and lots of coffee, he could hold out till Sunday, when Jess would leave.

For some reason, that prospect didn't appeal to him tonight the way it had yesterday. He wasn't so anxious anymore for the nosy reporter to take off again, even if that meant continuing to dodge the questions he didn't want to answer.

Of course, that was a dangerous state of mind. And due, no doubt, to those kisses at high noon. He found himself reliving those moments more often than he wanted to admit, and, even worse, anticipating a repeat experience.

Fortunately, when they drove up to the house, all the kids were outside after dinner. They'd set up a badminton net and were batting shuttlecocks back and forth. Even Justino and Lena had joined in the fun. Ford and Caroline were playing. Amber swooshed her racket around without actually hitting anything.

"I have to wait my turn," Garrett said as Dylan stepped onto the porch behind Jess. He nodded at the bag she carried. "What did you two buy?"

"Books," Jess announced with a grin. "Lots of books for teenagers. They can trade them around for a few weeks. There should be something for everybody to enjoy."

"That's a terrific idea." Garrett got to his feet and put his arms around her. "And a very generous donation on your part. Thanks so much."

She emerged from his hug with a blush in her cheeks. "Just creating my future audience, you know. Where should I put these out so the kids can sort through them?"

Garrett bore Jess off to the bunkhouse to set the

books out on the tables there. Dylan sank down into one of the rockers on the porch, suddenly too tired to do much more than watch other people having fun. When was the last full night's sleep he'd had?

"Hey, you." A hand shook his shoulder. "Wake up."

He opened his eyes. "I'm awake."

Wyatt snorted. "Sure. You were snoring."

"I never snore."

"You have three brothers who beg to differ."

Dylan knuckled his eyes. "They all snore."

"Maybe you ought to get some rest."

"I'm fine." He shook his head hard, trying for full consciousness. "All good."

Ford came to the edge of the porch. "I'm with the Boss. Get some sleep. We've got things covered till morning. Tomorrow we'll need you fully functional on the cattle drive."

"Jess—"

"Will manage the rest of the evening without your attention. She's over there with the kids, talking about books. We'll tell her you're working. Go to bed."

"Okay, okay. I give up." He almost tripped down the steps to the ground. "Shut up," he said, before anyone could remark on his lack of coordination. "I'll be up early tomorrow. Night."

At the studio, he considered lying down on an empty table rather than climbing up the stairs, but convinced himself to make the effort. Fortunately, he had an effective jack to help get his boots off. A second later, he put his head down on the pillow.

And smiled. The world's most famous scent still lingered from the morning when Jess had lain there.

Chanel. A sure ticket to sweet dreams.

JESS EXPECTED SOME of the grudging reactions from the kids with regard to the books. The usual suspects complained loud and long about first having to write something and now being expected to read. In contrast, though, Nate asked if he could take three books, Lizzie and Becky took two each, and Justino and Lena cooperated without comment.

What thrilled her, though, were the seven pieces of writing she received—one for every camper and all of them at least half a page. Each of them had made an effort. She couldn't wait to read what they'd come up with.

So she said good-night to the adults early and went to her room at the house, settled into the armchair with a cup of tea and began to read.

"I wud go to New York," wrote Marcos, "and ern mony to by stuf, like fast cars and tikets to ball games. I wud be real rich and not take crap from nobudy. I wud by my mom a house and she cud have people clene it for her all the time. And bring her tee to drink and make her food wen she wanted it and wash her dishs."

Blinking away tears, she pulled out Lena's page. "I would go to LA with Justino and we would become movie stars and wear butiful clothes and have a shofer to drive us from our butiful house in Beverly Hills to go shopping on Rodeo Drive. And my brothers would come live with us and go to privet schools and grow up to be smart so they could get good jobs in an office and wear sutes and not have to dig in the dirt to make money. I would send money to my dad so he could keep his tractor fixed and hire men to help him on the farm because my brothers are gone. And maybe he could find somebody to marry who would cook for him and take care of his house, like Mama did. And Justino and I would get to make movies all over the world and everybody would go see them because we are so butiful."

Jess pulled in a deep, shaking breath and thumbed through for Lizzie's paper. Since the girl had some writing experience, perhaps her piece would be more imaginative and not quite so wrenching.

Ten minutes later, Jess was striding through the quiet house and down the hill toward Dylan's studio. Even though he would be working, she couldn't wait to share Lizzie's composition with him. He would be as startled and as pleased as Jess was herself.

She reached the blue door and knocked briskly on one of the glass panes. "Dylan? Dylan, it's Jess."

When he didn't answer, she peered inside, but couldn't see him at the table where he'd worked last night, or at any of the others. He might be under the stairs, sketching. But surely, he would have heard her...

She rapped on the glass again. "Dylan!"

Then she saw him, barefoot and rumpled, coming down the stairs from the loft. He hadn't been working. He'd been sound asleep.

"I'm so sorry," she said, when he opened the door. "I thought—"

"What's wrong?" He rubbed a hand over his hair. "Somebody hurt?"

"No, no. I—"

"Glad to hear it." He nodded, a sexy, sleepy smile

curving his mouth. "Then I'll just go back to that terrific dream I was having."

Before she could react, he pulled her into his arms.
And then he covered her lips with his own.

Chapter Six

All the different sensations struck him at the same instant. Her hair tumbled over his forearms and the backs of his fingers like a waterfall, wild and untamed. That scent she wore surrounded him—floral with hints of citrus and spice but as cool as a blossom under snow. She felt small in his arms, thinner than she appeared and delicate, though he believed she possessed the strength to subdue a man.

Her mouth alone, full and sweet and agile, might very well be his undoing. He couldn't seem to get close enough, draw deep enough from the swell of emotion her lips evoked. The curve of her waist under his palm, the roundness of her bottom and the point of her shoulder blade offered pleasures he'd never understood until this night, this moment. Holding him tight around his waist, she pressed her body against his, and Dylan groaned low in his throat. A nip of her teeth, a buff of her tongue, and his knees dissolved.

This—*this*—was all he'd ever wanted, all he needed, this sense of belonging and rightness and *possibility* that they could find together. Just kissing, for God's sake. And when he had her naked, underneath him, sex with Jess was going to be the most incredible, consuming, inspiring…

Oh, jeez. What was he thinking?

Dylan stilled his hands and his mouth, and turned his head away from hers. He couldn't do anything about his fast breathing, or the pounding of his heart against her breasts.

"It was a great dream," he said, finally.

Jess hadn't moved. "I believe you."

He dropped his arms and retreated, feeling her hands slide over his belly as he moved away. "This seems to be my day for jumping your bones. I—"

She held up a hand. "No. Don't say you're sorry. I'm not."

He managed a smile. "That's nice to hear. What brought you over here?"

"I dropped it." She scanned the floor around them and picked up a piece of paper she found lying under the table. "I wanted you to read Lizzie's composition from this afternoon."

"Have a seat," he told her, taking the page she held. "Want some coffee?"

Jess shook her head. "No, thanks. I plan to sleep tonight. Maybe you should skip the caffeine, too. You look like you could use more rest."

"Caffeine doesn't keep me up." Which was a lie, or why else would he drink it? "Give me a minute to go through this."

Lizzie had written a poem.

In dreams I fly between the clouds and watch
from seagull's view

The rolling waves, loitering shells and roughly
sculpted sand.
Umbrellas, boldly striped, hide the day.
Bare bodies, oiled, catch the rays.
A wooden pier points out to sea, drawing fishes
to their doom,
But offering trinkets bright and sweet to lure a
human hand.
The scent of salt blooms on the wind.
I wake and mourn to be a girl again.

When he finished, he gazed at the woman in the
chair next to him. "Wow. Is it my imagination, or is
she really good?"

"I think she's exceptional for someone her age. I
can't believe her teachers would ignore this kind of
talent." She frowned. "Maybe, since Bisons Creek is
such a small town, the schools don't offer programs
to address gifted students."

"Caroline might be more of an expert on those issues. My guess would be Lizzie doesn't share with
very many people. But she knew you would read this
and she wanted you to be impressed." He handed the
page to Jess. "We've got the cattle drive tomorrow,
but maybe on Saturday you and she can do some serious talking. I'm sure your encouragement will mean
a lot to her."

"A couple of hours doesn't constitute much of an
effort." She frowned at the paper. "She needs consis-
tent support and feedback. I can imagine how much
that would have meant to me when I was her age."

"Maybe you and Caroline can talk to her together?
Then Caroline can stick with it after you've left."

"Yeah..." Jess left her chair and paced between the tables, her gaze sliding across his sculptures as if they weren't there. "There should be more I can do, though."

Dylan wasn't sure what else to say. The limitations to what she could accomplish in the time available were pretty obvious. She'd be gone by Sunday afternoon, which accounted for his current state of frustration, as well as hers.

At the far end of the room, Jess turned, and then stopped. She stood motionless, staring at nothing while Dylan took the chance to appreciate her beauty, as he had once appreciated the Venus de Milo. Jess Granger was even more glorious, however, for being alive.

"I want to stay," she said.

He sat up straight. "What?"

"I want to stay on the Circle M. Would that be possible?"

Dylan rubbed his eyes with the fingers of both hands. "I don't see why not. For Lizzie's sake?"

"For all the kids." She came returned sit beside him. "All of them could use help with their reading and writing. The rest of you are as busy as you can handle with the other projects you have going on and the ranch chores. My shifts with the kids would give you a break to get other work done, including your sculpture, so maybe you could get more sleep at night. It's the perfect answer."

"I hesitate to bring this up," Dylan said. "But don't you have a job? And what about the damn article? Wasn't there a deadline of some sort?"

"I can write the article here and email it to my editor. That's no problem. I probably would have been working on it at home, anyway. As for the job, well, I do have vacation. I think I could get the okay to use it now."

He stared at her. "That's not an offer I would have expected from someone in your position. I'm not even sure I'd have suggested it myself. I voted against the summer camp idea when Caroline proposed it."

"You had other priorities. And you have to admit that working with the kids takes your attention away from sculpture." Jess shrugged. "That's a hard choice to make."

Maybe. But right now, he was glad he'd lost that particular vote. "In any case, you are welcome to stay as long as you'd like, of course. I'm sure Caroline, Ford and Garrett will be glad to employ your energies in every way possible."

"I'm so excited." Her smile could have lit the room if he hadn't already switched on the lights. "This will be a lot of fun."

"I hope you say the same a week from now. First, though, you've got to get through the cattle drive. Are you riding Cash tomorrow?"

"I'm riding in the truck with Susannah and Wyatt. One lesson doesn't qualify me as a working cowgirl."

"You'd do fine." A huge yawn spoiled the effect of his compliment.

"You have seven kids to look after. That's enough for the four of you." She got to her feet. "And you ought to get some sleep. I'm sorry I woke you up."

"No problem. Just let me get my boots on and I'll walk you to the house." He headed for the stairs, and was surprised to find that Jess arrived at the bottom step with him.

She put a hand on his arm. "No. This is one of those moments when I'm asserting my independence. This isn't Central Park. I can walk myself to the house. You should go upstairs and climb into bed."

He discarded the first idea that occurred to him, an image of the two of them in bed together. "I can stay awake long enough—"

"No," she said again. "Go to bed. Alone," she continued, in answer to the lift of his eyebrow. "Sleep."

"All right. Can I walk you to the door?"

"I suppose." When they reached the designated area, she flipped the lights off. They stood in the dark, barely able to see each other. "Good night, Dylan." To his surprise, she reached up and kissed him lightly. "Sleep well."

Just that gentle touch set his body humming. "Sure. We'll be up and out early. Don't forget your hat."

"I wouldn't dare." She slipped out the door and closed it behind her, waved and then headed up the hill toward the house.

Dylan waited in the dark until he was more than sure Jess would have reached the house and gone inside. Then he flipped on the lights. He might be yawning, but his body remained full of tension, unable to relax. His brain buzzed between past and present, what had been and what could be. What *could* be, but...

Jess Granger was a self-sufficient woman who lived and worked in Manhattan, loved the big city and didn't like small towns. She shared the values of that world—values Dylan had deliberately forsaken when he came back home. A serious relationship between them could never succeed when their core beliefs were so starkly different.

And if he'd learned anything at all during his stint on the abstract art scene, surely he had learned the value of commitment and fidelity in relationships. Casual sex led to catastrophe, as far as Dylan was concerned. He wouldn't go down that road again.

Not even for someone as special as Jess.

THANKS TO THE time difference, Jess was able to catch her editor at work before Susannah and Wyatt were ready to leave and follow the cattle drive in the truck.

"Are you surviving out there in the hinterlands?" Sophia Accardi asked. "Has the wind whipped your skin raw?"

"Moisturizer is definitely a girl's best friend in Wyoming. But I'm near a town with a diner and a bookstore. Plus more handsome cowboys than I can count. What else do I need?"

"Do they chew tobacco?"

"No, Sophia. They don't smoke it, either, like some people." She'd nagged the other woman for years but had yet to convince her editor to drop the cigarette habit.

"Never mind that. All done? Ready to come home?"

Jess swallowed. "Um…getting there."

"I don't like the sound of 'getting there.' What's the problem? Have you or have you not discovered the answer to the question of what happened to Dylan Marshall?"

"I've discovered some of the answer."

"'Some' sounds evasive. Trevor Galleries wants

this article to make a big splash, Jess. They've paid big-splash money. You have to deliver big-splash content."

"I know."

"Otherwise, I'll find a writer who can. This is a business. I have to look at the bottom line."

"I understand." Jess took a deep breath. "While we're talking, can you okay a few days off for me? I need to stay…for the story."

"Your copy is due—"

"Yes, but Dylan Marshall is slow coming around. Give me the week. I'll come back with the truth." She was becoming pretty convincing at this lying thing.

"You'd better. We've had some good years together, sweetie. I'd hate to see it end."

The line went dead. Jess stared at her phone. "You're all heart."

Susannah came to her bedroom doorway carrying a basket of food, with Amber skipping along behind her. "We're ready if you are," she said.

"All set." Jess put her phone on the dresser and picked up her camera, smiling at the thought of leaving Sophia and *Renown Magazine* behind as she went out to enjoy the rest of her day.

An hour of travel along a web of gravel-and-dirt roads brought them to their rendezvous point with the cattle drive.

"The good thing about today's route," Wyatt said from the backseat as Susannah stopped the truck, "is that we can park here on the bluff overlooking the valley and watch them gather the cattle up along the river and push them on. We'll get kind of a wide-scale view of the process."

"Sounds like the perfect photo op. And I brought my zoom lens," Jess said, opening her door. "I can get close-ups as well as distance shots. How long will it be before we see them?"

"They'll come from the south end almost any moment now." Wyatt pointed to the left. "And exit to the right. We'll meet them for lunch just on the other side of those trees. It's a small pasture, ideal for holding this herd together while we eat."

"Do the kids understand what to do?" Susannah was keeping an eye on Amber, busy with her coloring book in the backseat of the truck. "There must be some skill involved in herding cows."

Wyatt got out and leaned against the grille of the truck. "The trick is to have a leader moving forward, and then using your wranglers to apply pressure from the sides to keep the animals moving. The cattle at the end of the line will want to keep up with the others that way. Ford will be at the head, with the kids on the sides. Garrett and Caroline can supervise, while Dylan will be riding at the rear in case of stragglers." He blew out a deep breath.

Jess noticed the sigh. "Would you be the leader if you were out there?"

"I usually bring up the tail. Dylan's a good man in front."

"When will you be able to get back to work?"

"On a horse, maybe Christmas." He winked at her. "Or when I get sick of sitting around. Whichever comes first."

She considered the implications. "So you'll be shorthanded through the summer and fall. That's a long time."

He nodded. "You're not kidding. Caroline's been taking up some of the slack while she's here for the camp, but she's supposed to be in her office, not herding cattle."

"That's right, Dylan mentioned she works for the Department of Family Services."

"And she has lots of clients to cover. Ford's still winding up his work for the law firm he left in San Francisco, plus handling legal cases in town, too. And Garrett's church requires his attention, of course. Nobody's covering just one job here right now, except me. And Dylan, I guess."

Jess looked at him hard. "You don't consider Dylan's art a job?"

Wyatt shrugged one shoulder. "I'd call it more of a hobby. A sideline."

"He made some pretty impressive money with that sideline." She tried to swallow her indignation. "Some of his art pieces sold for six figures."

"Money doesn't define what's important in life."

"Getting paid for work is generally the definition of a job. He'll be selling the work he's doing now, as well. Trevor Galleries is very eager to publicize this upcoming show."

"Which is why you're here. But what's your point, Ms. Granger? I'm pretty sure you've got one."

She pulled in a deep breath. "I'm surprised you treat something that means so much to your brother as a hobby."

His blue eyes were stern. "Dylan's a cowboy first and foremost. He'd tell you that himself."

"But is that the way he wants to live his life? Maybe

he'd like to be an artist who does ranch work as a hobby."

"That's not an option this summer." He glanced to the left. "There they come."

The noise struck her first—a hundred different versions of "moo," all sounding at once, and repeated time and time again. In protest? Or did cows just need to talk while they moved?

Then she could hear the other voices, as kids shouted "Hey!" and "Git" and "Yah." There were whistles in the mix, sharp and clear. Jess thought she could detect Caroline's voice among the other sounds, though she couldn't be sure.

Finally, she could distinguish Ford's light blue shirt at the front of...well, it looked like a big black cloud rolling along at his heels. A very noisy black cloud. As she watched, the cloud resolved into individual animals, black cows ambling forward, jostling and bumping each other, crowding together and shouldering their way through as they followed Ford on his bright gold horse. The horse's name was Nugget, he'd said, and the color was called palomino. Caroline's horse, Allie, was also palomino, but a darker shade. Jess could just make out Allie now, on the far side of the river of cattle. There were three other horses with her, but she couldn't tell the riders apart in their helmets.

On the near side, she found Garrett in his red shirt and four teenagers riding with him, doing pretty well at keeping the procession going forward.

"I can't figure out which one is Nate." Susannah had come to stand beside Jess, holding Amber in her arms. "Watch the cows, sweetie. Isn't that amazing, how they're all staying together? Nate's down there helping."

"Can I wave to him?"

Susannah laughed. "I don't think he'll see you. But you can try. We'll both wave."

Jess glanced at Wyatt, to share the humor of the moment with him, but found an expression of pain on his face, instead. Not physical pain, she thought, but emotional. As soon as he realized she was watching, however, his expression went blank.

He gave a brisk nod. "They're doing a good job."

Turning back to the scene, she lifted her camera and began taking pictures, trying to capture the action as faithfully as she could. With the telephoto lens, she found Becky on Caroline's side of the herd with Nate, both of the kids doing their best to keep the cows together. Lizzie, on her pony, Major, was farther away. The girl was making no effort to work with the others, which left Caroline shorthanded. Lena and Justino rode with Garrett, Thomas and Marcos.

Jess set her sight on Ford at the moment when he turned Nugget directly toward the river. "They're going across?" she asked, without losing her shot. "Is that dangerous?"

"Have the kids been through water before?" Susannah wanted to know.

"They're fine," Wyatt said, his voice calm and quiet. "The kids and the cows have been through water plenty of times. Don't worry."

The cows didn't seem quite as comfortable as he'd predicted. There were calves among the adults, and the little ones tended to balk. Or run away, which required a rider on a horse to bring them back. Caroline demonstrated how it was done as she sent Allie after an escaping calf and blocked its way until it rejoined the herd. Garrett took one on his side, and his black horse gleamed in the sunlight as he shifted in one direction and then another, convincing the calf to go with the flow.

Ford continued to ride forward, and most of the cows seemed to be following him and Nugget. The water in the creek was only up to the horses' knees, and once the cattle realized this, most seemed to understand the best way to go was through the middle. With the exception of Lizzie, the kids on each side kept the pressure on, and with Garrett and Caroline chasing strays, the process seemed to be a success.

Jess finally located Dylan at the tail end of the drive. Working actively to keep the stragglers on both sides from wandering off, his pony moved like a dancer, swaying and jumping as necessary to do the job. Sitting straight and tall, Dylan appeared to be in complete control, always a step ahead of the cattle he tended.

But then Wyatt straightened up. "Damn."

"What's wrong?" Jess and Susannah asked at the same time.

"They're falling out on Caroline's side. Not enough pressure."

As if a pipe had sprung a leak, the remaining cows on the far side of the creek were refusing to go into the water, and instead started trotting beside the stream. In an instant, the cows on Ford's side had started running, as well. Dust roiled in the air, and the only sound was the thunder of hundreds of hooves. All the horses were now speeding up, while two black torrents of cows stampeded toward the north end of the valley and a four-board fence in front of a wall of trees.

The only thing in their way was Nugget, with Ford on his back.

Galloping just ahead of the cows on his tail, Ford sent Nugget into the creek again, directly across the path of the original runaways. As if bent by his will, the flow of animals curved just shy of the fence, turning in upon itself to become a slowly milling congregation of unhappy, but uninjured, cattle.

Wyatt took off his hat and wiped his forehead with his shirtsleeve. "The boy is good. I'll give him that."

Watching through her lens, Jess said, "Wait. Somebody's on the ground."

Susannah stood at her shoulder. "Can you tell who?"

"I can't find the horse. It went into the trees on the hill." She brought the camera up and focused the lens, scanning until she found Dylan kneeling on the ground beside a prone figure.

"Lizzie," she said, feeling hollow inside. "Lizzie fell off."

DYLAN SAW THE moment when the drive started to go wrong, but there wasn't much he could do to stop a train from behind. He figured Ford would turn them in on themselves and end the run. His big brother was talented that way.

The problem was seven kids in the middle of a cattle stampede. Horses tended to bolt when the cows did—they were all herd animals and reacted instinctively. Most of the teenagers could probably handle the situation and would sit back, relax and keep their heels down. They'd stay in the saddle okay.

But Lizzie was a nervous rider at best. As long as Major, her pony, did exactly what she expected, she was happy. If he made any sudden move, she panicked.

And so Dylan was watching when Major took off, just like the rest of the horses. Lizzie did all the wrong things—hunched her shoulders and jerked on the reins, giving Major something to pull against and a reason to keep running. Her hands came up and she wobbled in the saddle. Then, with a scream you could hear above the cow noise, she went down.

He threw himself off Leo and landed beside her on his knees, panting. "Lizzie? Lizzie, can you hear me? Are you okay?" He put a hand on her shoulder, brushing her blond hair away from her face. "Say something, sweetie."

"It hurts."

"What hurts? Your arm? Your leg?" She lay on her side, and he wasn't sure he should move her.

"Everything." She sniffed. "I want to go home."

"We need to make sure you're all right, first. Can you wiggle your fingers and toes?"

Eyes closed, she wiggled her fingers. The toes of her boots moved. "Yeah."

"How about your hands and feet? Your arms and legs? Do those move?"

He checked her over and couldn't see any obvious bone breaks. "Let me help you sit up, sweetie."

"It'll hurt."

That was probably true. "But you don't want to

lie here in the grass. We want to get you someplace more comfortable."

With a lot of coaxing, he got her on her feet. He thought she might have twisted her wrist. "How about getting up on Major again? Miss Caroline found him and brought him back. He's sorry he ran off. The cows spooked him."

"No!" She jerked away from Dylan's hold, which indicated an overall lack of injuries on Lizzie's part. "I never want to be on a horse again. I want to go home."

Caroline rode up, holding Major's reins. "You can't walk, Lizzie. It's too far."

"I can go in the truck. It's right up there."

"Are you going to climb the cliff? They can't drive down here."

The girl put her face in her hands and started to cry. Dylan stared at Caroline and shrugged. "She could get on behind you."

They finally convinced Lizzie to ride Allie with Caroline, but only to the site where they would eat lunch. *Then* she would never get on a horse again.

Dylan signaled to Wyatt to move the truck to meet up with Caroline and Lizzie. Ponying Major alongside Leo, he helped Ford and Garrett get the cattle drive to move forward again. He'd stayed up until after three sanding wood last night, but at least with all the action going on, he wouldn't risk falling asleep in the saddle.

The cows didn't like going through the creek any better the second time, but the wranglers' tempers had gotten shorter with the setbacks and their voices firmer, so the whole herd made it across without losing any more calves or personnel. Ford led them through the gate in the fence, the boys and Becky and Lena kept a strong presence along the sides of the string, and Dylan pushed the very last of those dogies straight through into the lunch pasture.

"And all we have to do after this is repeat the process," he told Jess as he sat down beside her on the log she'd chosen. "Minus the creek. We don't have to cross water again today."

"You look tired." She frowned at him. "Something tells me you didn't go back to bed last night."

He grinned at her. "That would be the problem. One way or another."

She frowned harder. "I would punch you but I have a sandwich in one hand and a drink in the other."

"I'll consider it done. Did you get some good pictures?"

"Loads of great shots, till the drama took over. Do you think Lizzie really wants to go home?"

"At this moment, she does. The shock of hitting the ground is a jolt to your emotions as well as your body. She's been so careful, she hasn't come off before this. Maybe when she realizes she's not hurt, she'll calm down."

"The rest of the kids managed pretty well."

"Most of them have fallen at least once. Even Nate. Sometimes being too careful works against you. Taking a fall can boost your confidence."

Jess turned her head and their eyes met. Dylan heard the echo of what he'd just said, saw the same recognition go through her mind. The moment went still—no wind, no chattering kids, no bawling cattle, just the two of them alone, acknowledging a new understanding.

Ford produced one of his piercing whistles, and the silence broke. "Time to get lunch cleaned up so we can move on," he announced. "Make sure all your trash gets to the truck."

Dylan shook his head, put his hands on his knees and pushed himself upright. "What the trail boss says is law. I'll take your trash."

But, as usual, she had to be independent about the issue. "I can manage." She walked with him to the truck. "You're going to be short a helper—"

"Wrangler, we call them."

"Short a wrangler. And there's an extra horse. Will that be a problem on the rest of the trip?"

"It's definitely less than ideal. We could move these cows with three or four experienced people, but keeping an eye on the kids and the cattle complicates the process. I do have an idea about how to solve one problem, though. If you're willing."

"Me?"

"You could ride Major. The pony Lizzie was on."

She laughed. "You want to put me on a horse somebody else fell off of? The prospect doesn't thrill me."

"Lizzie fell off because she panicked. You won't do that. Will you?"

Again, their gazes held. "No, I don't think I would. He's a good horse?"

"The best. And you'd be a big help. It's more fun than riding in the truck, too."

"Now, that's a solid argument. Okay, I'm game. Do I have to wear a helmet?"

"Yes. Wouldn't want to damage that high-powered brain of yours."

"You said I wouldn't fall off."

"Does your magazine have a lawyer on staff?"

"Yes."

"You're definitely wearing a helmet."

Once she'd climbed into Major's saddle, Dylan realized he'd have to lengthen the stirrups. "You're quite a bit taller than Lizzie. We'll have to make some adjustments." He put a hand on her knee. "Bring your leg forward so I can get to the straps."

So there he was, with Jess's slender, shapely thighs right at face level, trying to keep his mind on buckles and straps. "Can you bring your foot down so I can see how long…that's right." He cleared his throat. "Now stand up in the stirrups, and forgive the intrusion, but—" There was no way to tell how far off the seat she was except by touch, so he slipped his hand between her legs. It had to be his most awkward moment with a woman. Ever.

Dylan stepped back quickly. "Okay, you're set. Just keep your heels down and your chin up. You'll do great." Jess's cheeks looked as red as his felt. To avoid her gaze, he turned to Leo and swung himself into the saddle. "As they used to say on TV—head 'em up and move 'em out!"

Garrett took over the tail end of the drive. Marcos moved over to work with Nate and Becky, while Justino, Lena and Thomas stayed with Dylan and Jess. Ford threaded the leaders through the gate and the procession restarted, with the uphill portion of the trip ahead of them.

Despite his confident talk, Dylan worried that a

cattle drive wasn't the optimal setting for Jess's second experience on horseback, but she proved him wrong. She took a few minutes to get used to Major's gait, which was shorter and faster than Cash's, but once settled she became a working part of the team. She kept Major close to the herd, applying the pressure they needed to move the cattle forward. And she did it with a smile, clearly enjoying the adventure. Her cheerful attitude infected Thomas, who'd done his work with a scowl most of the morning, as well as Lena's and Justino's outlooks. The afternoon became the fun experience they'd hoped it would be for the kids, at least on his side. All thanks to a snobby journalist from New York.

They reached their destination at about three in the afternoon. Ford opened the gate to the pasture but then circled around behind to help push the cows through rather than lead them. Recognizing the cool green grass they'd been craving all day long, the calves and their mamas trotted straight across the field for as long as they could stand before coming to a dead stop and starting to graze. After all the effort, the day turned peaceful as the humans sat on their horses and simply watched the result of their labors.

"So how do we get back?" Thomas asked. "Is somebody coming to pick us up?"

Dylan looked at him. "You're sitting on your transportation."

Marcos groaned. "Man, my butt is tired," he whined. "I gotta get off."

Lena didn't say anything, just took her feet out of the stirrups and slid down from her horse. "I have to walk around. My legs are all cramped."

"We can break for a few minutes," Ford conceded. "Caroline's got candy bars in her saddle bag and Garrett carried water. We'll all feel better with a snack."

And they did, for a while. But at the end of the day, when five adults and six teenagers rode their horses up the hill and stopped outside the barn, determining who was the most exhausted would have been a challenge. Dylan had found himself falling asleep in the saddle more than once on the way back, to the point that Jess had reached over and pushed him up straight, afraid he was going to fall off the horse. Fortunately, they were almost home at that point. He contemplated skipping dinner and going straight to bed. Then his stomach growled, reminding him that he should eat, too.

They all led their horses into the corral and were parked around the fence, slowly removing saddles, bridles and blankets, when Wyatt emerged from the barn. Dylan was bringing Jess's saddle to the tack room, and so was within earshot when his oldest brother spoke with Ford and Caroline.

"Lizzie called home and no one answered. She reached her dad on his cell phone. Her parents are in Las Vegas."

Caroline gasped. "They didn't inform me they would be leaving town. When are they coming back?"

"That's just it," Wyatt said. "She told them she wants to leave the ranch. Today."

Ford lifted an eyebrow. "And they said…"

"They have a room reserved for three weeks. They'll be home 'sometime' after that."

Garrett had heard, too. "Who's listed on her paperwork to call in case of emergency?"

"Her aunt." Wyatt cleared his throat. "She and her husband are in Vegas, too. There's nobody left in Bisons Creek to take Lizzie in."

Dylan filled in the blanks. "Except, of course, for us."

Chapter Seven

"Not bad for an older woman."

Jess glanced over as Dylan put his dinner plate on the table and sat down next to her. "Thanks. I think."

"You are thirty-five, after all. Who knew you still had it in you to wrangle cattle?"

To celebrate their cattle drive accomplishments, the teenagers had been given the night off from cooking. Ford had grilled steaks and ears of corn while Susannah had baked potatoes and thrown together a big salad. Dessert would be the chocolate cake she and Lizzie had spent the afternoon baking. Now everyone had settled at the long table in the bunkhouse to enjoy the meal.

Jess gave Dylan a dirty look. "You're asking for trouble, cowboy. I have that article to write up, remember. Insult me, and I'll get even."

He sighed and rested his head on his hand, poking at his steak with his fork. "Yeah, we still have that to deal with, don't we? Couldn't you just write about the camp instead?"

"Not unless you want to explain to Trevor Galleries why they're not getting the punch for their advertising dollars."

"The one time I spoke with Patricia Trevor, she struck me as a person who keeps a close watch on her bank balance. In fact..." Sitting up straight, he cut a piece of meat, but didn't eat it. "In fact, I wondered why she called me in the first place. She doesn't usually feature Western art. She's more interested in glitz and glamour, from what I've seen of her ads. But she said my reputation alone would bring in business. I guess that's where you come in with this blasted article."

"Since the new gallery she's opening is in Denver, maybe she expects Western themes to be more popular here."

"Could be. Of course, Denver considers itself pretty sophisticated."

Jess eyed his plate. "Why aren't you eating?" When had she started worrying about him? And why? He had three brothers to do that.

"I'm too damn tired. And too damn hungry not to."

As a distraction, she glanced at the girl huddled over her plate at the end of the table, also not eating. "I wish I could say I'm surprised that Lizzie's parents would leave without telling anyone." With a sigh, Jess forked up a mouthful of potato and butter. "But I've seen much worse."

"Not lived it, I hope."

She glanced around to gauge who might be listening. Not that she had secrets, after yesterday afternoon's confession. "I was usually safe. But then, Lizzie is safe. I bet she feels abandoned, though. And that's cruel."

"But the other girls will help her out. Caroline is here. And you're staying, which will give her something else to focus on. Maybe she can consider this her own private writing retreat."

"Anything I can do." She smiled, but then remembered she hadn't yet canceled her return reservation to New York. "By the way, you haven't noticed my phone lying on a table somewhere in the house, have you?"

"No, but I can check more closely. It's not in the kitchen or living room?"

"Not that I saw. I talked to my editor this morning before we left and got the okay to stay out here for a week, as long as the article came in on deadline. I remember putting the phone down on the dresser in my room, but it's not there. I figured I wouldn't need it on the cattle drive."

"Service out there isn't reliable, anyway. And the cows drown out most other sounds."

"I noticed." She also noticed that he'd pushed his plate away with only half his dinner finished.

He noticed her noticing. "After all the calories Susannah has been feeding us, I don't expect to be wasting away anytime soon."

"I'm sure I won't." Her cheeks heated up at being caught watching out for him. "My jeans will all be too tight when I get back to New York."

"I doubt the guys there will complain."

Rolling her eyes, she stood up from her chair. "I'll take your plate if you're finished. Do you want cake?"

"Is that a rhetorical question? It's chocolate."

"Right."

Friday night, Jess had learned, was movie night, when the kids were allowed to watch television from dinner until bedtime. Tonight's movies were science fiction, which landed at the bottom of her preference list. She was prepared to be polite, but as she dried dishes while Dylan watched, she discovered she didn't have to.

"I'm not a sci-fi fan," he confessed, handing her a salad bowl. "Ugly monsters bursting out of people's chests? No, thanks."

"What would you rather watch?"

"Cowboy movies, which they're not making too often these days. Or anything historical—pirates, gladiators, even World War II. The more accurate, the better."

Jess dried the bowl without responding. How could something as simple as a movie preference set her pulse racing? So they shared a taste in films. Big deal. Anyway, movies based on Jane Austen books probably did not fall under Dylan's "historical" category.

He passed her the serving platter. "I even enjoyed the films they made from Jane Austen's books. Not much action, but there's something so beautiful about England. And, of course, there are the horses. I'm a sucker for a movie with horses."

Jess dropped the platter, which shattered on the concrete floor. "Oh, damn! I'm so sorry!" She hunkered down to pick up the pieces.

"Stop, we'll get a broom." He put a hand on her shoulder. "Really, Jess, you're going to get—"

As he said it, she hissed at the sudden slice of glass across her palm. "You're right. I am."

Caroline came up with a broom. "You two move out of the way so I can sweep this up." She saw Jess holding a paper towel to her hand. "You got cut? Poor thing. There's a big first aid kit at the house. Can you make it there with the paper towel? Just go on, now. I've got this."

Dylan went with her, keeping his arm around her waist as if she might faint. "It's not that bad," she assured him. "Just a shallow cut."

He shuddered. "That sounds terrible. I'm not so good with blood."

She laughed at him. "Then why did you come?"

"Moral support."

But in fact, when they got to the ranch house kitchen, he pulled out the first aid kit and took over the bandaging process. "This is deeper than you said."

"It's practically stopped bleeding already." His fingertips were warm on her skin.

"Do you see your phone, while you're sitting there doing nothing?"

"No. I can use my computer for now. But I do need my phone."

Dylan smoothed the tape over her palm. "I guess you won't be riding for a few days. It's lucky we had our cattle drive today, since we needed your help." He was still holding her hand in both of his, rubbing his thumb lightly over the back of her wrist.

She was starting to get chills from the contact. Pulling away, she said, "Let me go check the living room. Maybe I just don't remember what I did with the phone."

"I'll check the studio," Dylan said, after they'd searched underneath all the cushions and pillows. Honey followed them around the room, as if maybe she could sniff out what they couldn't find otherwise. "It could be there and I just didn't notice it. I don't keep track of my phone most of the time."

When Jess sat down on the rocker, the dog planted herself at her knee, clearly expecting to be petted. "I'm beginning to understand why people have animals. It's very soothing to stroke their heads, have them lean against you."

Dylan sat forward with his elbows on his knees and his hands clasped. "You could have a dog of your own, couldn't you? Or a cat. They're more self-sufficient. Like you."

"Are there cats on the Circle M? I haven't seen one."

"We have barn cats. They keep the mice away. But they tend to be pretty shy."

Shaking her head, Jess relaxed into the chair. "I doubt I'm home enough to keep an animal. I go out of town for several days at least every six weeks on interviews. What would the poor dog or cat do then?"

"One of your friends would stop by and keep them company," Dylan said. "It would be good for both of them."

"I'm not sure there's anybody who would do that for me. I suppose there are services you can hire. But then you've got a stranger coming into your house when you're not there. It sounds too complicated to me."

"Your life sounds too solitary to me."

She sat up straight and stared at him. "I'm here to talk about your life, not mine."

"You can't have one without the other."

"That's ridiculous. Of course I can. I'm a journalist."

"Not with me."

"I'm not a journalist with you? What does that mean?"

"In my opinion, we've progressed to being friends. Even more than friends."

"Dylan—" The problem was, she couldn't deny the truth. How had this gone so wrong?

"And that gives me the right to be concerned. You don't seem to have a man in your life, and you don't have friends who would come over to take care of a pet. You don't have a family to depend on. Is there anybody in your life you care about? Anybody to care about you?"

"I have friends."

"Have you called them, since you've been here? Have they called to make sure you arrived?"

"We get together when I'm in town."

"Who do you call to bring you medicine when you're sick?"

"I have a pharmacy that delivers."

"Well, that's great." He slapped his hands on his thighs and stood up. "Do they deliver chicken soup, too?"

"That's the Chinese place down the block." Jess smiled at him as she left the rocking chair. "It's nice of you to worry about me. But I've lived on my own for more than fifteen years. I'm an expert."

"You shouldn't have to be." He came to stand in front of her, putting his hands on her shoulders. "Everybody needs someone to take care of them."

"And what happens when that *someone* leaves? Or changes their mind? Or dies? Relationships always end, Dylan. What are you supposed to do then?"

"Not always. But if they do, you keep going. You find somebody else."

She shook her head. "Thanks, but I'm satisfied depending on the one person I'm certain will always stick around—myself." Stepping away from his hands, she walked to the door of the hallway. "I'm going to get my plane ticket changed, and then turn in early. I'm pretty tired after that ride this afternoon."

"I'll bring your phone over if I find it," he promised, his handsome face solemn, his dark eyes sad. "See you in the morning."

Jess didn't wait to watch him leave, but walked down the hallway to her room and closed the door firmly behind her. All these people with their smiles and good intentions had diminished her detachment. A few hours of solitude would restore her objectivity and balance. She hoped.

Crossing the room, she reached for her leather tote bag, which carried her computer as well as every other possession she might conceivably need if the airline lost her suitcase. When she picked it up, the unexpected lightness caught her attention and she stood it up on the bed, spreading the handles to peer inside.

The computer was missing, along with its power cord. And the remaining contents of the bag were wrecked. Makeup had been pulled out of the toiletries bag and left lying open, with eye shadow, mascara and face powder now streaking the silk lining of the tote. The papers in her wallet and the notebook she always carried had been pulled out and scattered through the bag. The wallet itself was missing.

Swearing softly, Jess fetched a towel from the bathroom and spread it over the bed, then upended the tote over it and shook hard. The disturbed contents tumbled onto the towel, along with a dribble of pink moisturizer and the bottle, from which the cap had been removed.

"It's ruined," she muttered. "Totally destroyed."

Feeling sick to her stomach, she sorted through the articles on the towel, making a pile for the trash, one for makeup she could still use and another for the items that were supposed to be in her wallet.

"I've been robbed," Jess said aloud. "Vandalized and robbed."

THE KITCHEN WAS crowded when Dylan strode into the house on Saturday morning. "Call the sheriff," he said loudly. "My studio has been vandalized."

They all straightened up, and Jess gasped. "Dylan, no!"

"Pieces knocked over and thrown around, tools bent, mangled, scattered. He set a fire on the floor, for God's sake. All my sketches, burnt to a crisp. I didn't switch on the light last night so I didn't see it. Not till this morning." He was breathing hard. "The wooden pieces didn't burn well, so I guess he gave up. Or didn't have time. I can't believe this. Who would do such a thing?"

"He was here, too," Wyatt said. "Jess has been robbed."

Dylan stared at her. "Your phone?"

"My wallet, cash and credit cards," she said. "The computer and the phone."

"Damn, I'm sorry. That's a hell of a thing to happen. Though not," he said, turning back to Ford, "entirely unexpected. Have you talked to the kids?"

"Not yet. There's nothing to indicate one of the teenagers knows anything about this."

Coffee splashed out of several mugs when Dylan pounded his fist on the counter. "Who else?"

"All of us—including the kids—were away from the ranch yesterday. Someone could easily have come in and taken whatever they wanted."

"For the first time in twenty years? Come on, Ford, isn't that a little naive?"

Carolyn stepped forward. "Let's take a wider view, Dylan. Just because something hasn't happened in the past doesn't mean it didn't happen yesterday."

He met her bright green gaze. "I hate that one of the kids might have betrayed our trust. But it seems the most likely answer. They could have told someone we'd be gone—the perfect setup." Shaking his head, he finished wiping up the spilled coffee. "So I take it we won't be going to the rodeo this afternoon."

Garrett poured himself another mug. "Why not? We aren't going to spend the day interrogating the kids with thumbscrews and branding irons."

"You have to talk to them, at least."

"We'll talk to each one individually," Ford said. "But before you even ask, I don't intend to search everyone's bags."

Jess said, "I agree. These aren't hardened criminals. They won't be able to lie convincingly."

Dylan started to say something smart, but stopped himself. They'd come to this conclusion without him, so there was no point in protesting. "What about your files, Jess? Are they backed up?"

She nodded. "I save everything online, so I can retrieve my work."

"That's smart of you." He looked at Wyatt. "Is anything else missing?"

His brother nodded. "Beer from the fridge. My phone and my computer, which I'd left on my dresser. Garrett's computer is at the church and Ford had locked his in his truck. We didn't have money lying around, besides Jess's. Most of the electronics are too big to carry easily or hide."

"How about the tack room? We've got silver spurs in there, silver conchas decorating a couple of saddles..."

"Everything's where it should be." Ford's hand came down on his shoulder. "Just try to calm down. It's especially terrible that this happened to a guest in the house. We'll be replacing the cash and the phone—"

"No, you won't," Jess said.

"Yes, we will," the lawyer insisted. "And maybe we'll figure out who did this and get it all back. But until then, we carry on with the day as planned. We'll just be sure the house is locked tight this afternoon while we're gone."

"I'm staying," Wyatt said. "I've been to my share of rodeos."

"Even better," Ford said. "Now, Dylan, let's go check out your studio before we have to get the kids working on breakfast."

As his brothers and Caroline walked ahead, Dylan kept pace with Jess. "I can't believe we're still going to the rodeo. The least we could do is stay home until the sheriff has come out."

She held her hands out in a helpless gesture. "What can they do? The stuff has been gone since yesterday afternoon."

"Something, at least—we could examine tire tracks, take casts of footprints. I have some plaster in the studio."

"Right, Sherlock. I think locking the door when you leave is the best strategy I've heard all morning."

"We've never had to do that before." He hesitated at the entrance to the studio. "Do you suppose it's just coincidence that this happens during the same summer we have seven adolescent troublemakers staying with us?"

Jess didn't say anything, but he could read her face. Dylan nodded. "Yeah, me, neither."

Ford and Garrett and Caroline condemned the damage in his workshop. "This is terrible," Ford said. "I hate seeing your sculpture attacked like this."

"That's three pieces I have to replace in the inventory for the showing in November," Dylan told him. "I'm supposed to produce twenty-five individual sculptures, and I was going to have to push to get the last two done. I don't know how I can possibly work up three replacements." He pushed his hair back from his face. "If I don't have enough to show they might cancel the whole event."

Jess gazed at him, speechless with distress. But the worst part for Dylan was that he couldn't move anything, couldn't pick up his sculptures and see how bad the damage was, until after a deputy had examined the scene. Witnessing his studio as a crime scene made him sick to his stomach.

With seven kids to take care of, though, the morning soon resumed its standard routine—breakfast in the bunkhouse followed by general house cleanup for both the boys and the girls. Complaints were lodged, as usual, but somehow the necessary tasks got done, even though the kids disappeared one after the other to talk with Ford, Caroline and Jess.

And the results, as Dylan had predicted, weren't useful. "They lie better than you expected them to," he said, when the adults reassembled in the kitchen at noon. "Should have used the thumbscrews."

"Or else they didn't do it," Garrett pointed out, frowning. He seemed to be frowning a lot lately. "Innocent until proven guilty?"

"We called the sheriff's office," Ford said. "Wade Daughtry said he'd investigate who from the outside might have done this."

Dylan rubbed the nape of his neck, where a headache had started. "And you still plan to go to the show this afternoon?"

"Maybe it's for the best." When he sent her an incredulous look, Jess said, "Why sit here stewing about it, waiting for the deputy? We can all use a diversion. It'll be my first and probably only rodeo." Then it was her turn to frown. "But somebody will have to pay my way."

Dylan put an arm around her waist and squeezed. "I'll be honored to take you as my date."

"This isn't a date. I'll repay you." She glared at him. "And we can talk about your rodeo days for the article."

As they gathered to load up for the trip to Buffalo, however, Caroline walked down from the girls' cabin with a harried expression on her face. "Lizzie is refusing to go."

"She enjoyed it the last time," Dylan said. "What's different?"

"A fall," Garrett told him. "And her whole attitude."

"I can stay home with her," Caroline said. "Maybe we can talk and I can persuade her to stay in the program." Her glance at Ford was loaded with regret.

"Or I could," Jess said. "I wanted to meet with her about her writing, anyway."

"You'd miss the rodeo," Dylan protested. "Our date."

"It was not a date," Jess insisted. "This is more important."

"I'd hate to have you pass up the show," Caroline said. "I wonder if Lizzie would go if she could ride in the car with you and talk about writing."

Jess nodded. "I'll ask."

While she was gone, the boys and Lena climbed into the van they were using to transport the kids. Dylan remained outside with Ford and Garrett.

"This is a hell of a thing to have happen," he told them. "I knew there would be trouble when we brought those kids to the ranch."

"If you say that a little louder they'll be sure to hear you," Garrett snapped. "The theft is not related to the kids."

"Neither of you is sure of your facts," Ford said in a taut voice. "And having you argue about this doesn't help. Dylan, why don't you ride with Caroline and Jess? You'll agitate the situation if you ride with us and the guys."

"Not a problem for me." Dylan walked to his truck, where Caroline and Becky were waiting. "Where's Susannah?"

"She decided to stay home. Amber wasn't too happy about going to a rodeo. I think she has some bad memories from when her dad would act out after he lost." Nate's dad was a cowboy and perennial loser at bull riding.

"Poor little girl." He glanced at the girls' cabin and saw Jess and Lizzie coming down the hill. "We've got Lizzie on board, anyway. Let's climb in. The show starts in just under an hour."

With Caroline riding shotgun and Jess, Lizzie and Becky in the backseat, Dylan followed the van off the ranch. The rearview mirror showed the blonde girl huddled in on herself in the middle, with her friend staring out the window on one side and the journalist on the other. Jess caught him watching and gave a tiny shrug. He nodded in encouragement, and made a thumbs-up sign for good measure.

"So, Lizzie," she started, "I really liked the poem you wrote on Thursday. Do you write poems often?"

Shrug.

"You painted a lovely picture of a day at the beach. Have you been to the beach?"

Head shake. And then, when an answer seemed unlikely, "I want to go."

"I went once," Becky said. "In California. The water was cold."

"Did Lizzie show you her poem?"

"Yeah. But my favorite is the one about horses."

"Did you write about the horses when you came to camp?"

Nod.

"I'd be glad to read that one. This is my first experience with horses, too."

"I ripped it up."

Caroline gasped, and Becky made a sound of protest. Dylan tightened his grip on the steering wheel.

Jess stayed calm. "Yeah, sometimes when you're angry it feels good to tear up something you wrote about. Kind of like revenge."

"Yeah."

"Did it make you happy?"

"Not really."

"When I rip up my work, I end up feeling as if I punished myself. Usually, no one else finds out. And wouldn't care if they did."

Lizzie sighed. "Horses are stupid."

Dylan couldn't stay quiet. "In some ways, they are, but not always. Can you imagine what would happen if a horse—especially a short one like Major—stood still while the herd ran toward him?"

This pause lasted so long he was sure he'd made a huge mistake.

Finally, though, she answered. "He'd get run over."

"He would. You would, too, if you were in the saddle."

Another extended silence. "So he was protecting me."

"He was staying safe the only way he knew how. We depend on horses to do that and try to anticipate danger. You just weren't quite ready for his reaction. He didn't mean to dump you. Believe me, I've ridden horses that tried, and they're very good at it."

"In the rodeo?"

"And at the ranch. You can get a horse with a bad attitude. But Major is not one of those horses." He waited a moment. "I think you know that."

"Yeah."

He looked into the mirror and nodded to Jess. *Back to you.*

"What else have you written about?" Jess asked. "Do you write stories? Make up characters and follow them through their adventures?"

"She writes about a girl wizard," Becky said. "Her hair changes color when she does magic."

"Shut up," Lizzie told her. "She'll think it's silly."

"If you enjoy it, it isn't silly," Jess promised her. "Tell me more about this wizard."

Lizzie wouldn't, but Becky had obviously enjoyed the story and shared the details as they finished the drive to Buffalo. If there was a resemblance to certain wildly popular books already in print, Dylan decided there were enough differences to make the story impressive.

"When you're a published author, you'll have to come to Bisons Creek and do book signings," he said to Lizzie as they got out of the truck. "We'll all be proud to say we knew you when."

She gave him a shy smile. "I will."

"But for now, we have to help Ms. Jess enjoy the rodeo. This is a youth event," he explained to the woman in question. "For kids eighteen and under. Not quite as dangerous as the grown-up version, and sometimes a lot funnier." Because it was the Fourth of July, the arena was decorated with red, white and blue bunting. American flags fluttered wherever you looked, and patriotic balloons had been tied to every available post. The music blaring over the loudspeaker was dedicated to home and country.

Jess surveyed the holiday crowd. "So this is the kind of rodeo the campers might want to enter?"

Ford and Garrett joined them, with the boys trailing along behind. "Our hope is to sponsor a local youth rodeo at the end of the summer," Ford said, "giving everybody a chance to compete."

Dylan stared at him. "I hadn't heard about that. When did you come up with this idea?"

Caroline put a hand on his arm. "It's still just an idea, Dylan. We haven't made any definite arrangements."

"You didn't think I might want to be included in the discussion?" His brothers and Caroline exchanged guilty looks. "What did Wyatt say?"

"He's supportive..." Garrett's voice trailed off.

"But you assumed I wouldn't be. Hmm, wonder why?" He shook his head. "This is turning out to be a very interesting day." Gazing around a bit blindly, he found Jess standing beside him and grabbed her hand. "We'd better get to the stands. Lamb-bustin' is about to start."

"Lamb-bustin'?" she echoed. "What in the world is that?"

"Junior league bull riding. Young kids start out riding lambs. They don't buck much and they're close to the ground."

"Do the sheep mind?"

"No animal enjoys having someone on its back— that's basically like being prey. But they don't get hurt. And sheep aren't all that smart, so I doubt the trauma lasts."

"What a crazy world this is."

The boys headed up to the top of the stands to find a place to sit. With Jess's hand still in his, Dylan followed them and took seats as far away from the rest of his family as he could manage. Lizzie and Becky sat on Jess's other side.

"Are you throwing a tantrum?" Jess asked him. "Will it make a difference?"

"Yes. And probably not." Dylan shrugged. "They mean well."

"They don't seem to take your sculpture very seriously. They regard it as something to be done after every other chore has been taken care of."

"That worked okay when we didn't have seven kids on the premises. Now that we do, something has to give."

"Actually, I argued with Wyatt about this yesterday, before lunch."

"You did? Why?"

"I told him I'm surprised that he takes your dedication to your sculpture so lightly. He described it as a hobby, or a sideline."

"Ouch." Not that he was surprised. "A man of the land, our Wyatt is."

"But you stay here. You could go to a place where your art was taken seriously."

"This is my home. They're my family."

The first event in the arena was, of course, the flag ceremony, with a pretty blonde girl in red, white and blue riding her Appaloosa horse around the ring, carrying a big American flag. As "The Star-Spangled Banner" blared from the announcer's booth, the crowd stood and joined in on the words. A glance at the kids beside him showed Dylan that most of them were mumbling along, though Thomas and Marcos, of course, remained scornfully quiet.

"Now for the action," Dylan said when the crowd sat down again.

A little girl riding on the back of a sheared lamb

started out across the arena, only to slip off about half-way. Laughing, Dylan squeezed Jess's hand without letting go. "Who would want to miss this?"

She grinned. "It is pretty funny."

But her eyes were worried.

As soon as the lamb-busting ended, the teenaged boys started clamoring for something to eat and drink. With a glance at Jess, Dylan volunteered the two of them to supervise the process. They followed the kids down to the food aisle, where they all scattered to different stands in search of their favorite treats.

"What would you like?" he asked Jess. "Fried cookies or pickles? Pigs feet on a bun?"

"How about some ice cream?"

"Perfect."

As they stood at the corner of the bleachers, licking chocolate-covered cones and waiting for the crew of teens to return from their forays, Jess suddenly sent him a piercing look.

"What?" he said. "Do I have chocolate on my chin?"

"Yes, as a matter of fact." She reached up with a napkin and wiped his face. "But I was wondering if you remember that you owe me."

"What do I owe you?"

"The answer to one probing, self-immolating question."

"Oh, that."

"Yes, damn it. That."

He took a deep breath and blew it out. "Okay. Go for it."

She hesitated, staring at him, her brows lowered in concentration.

"My ice cream is melting," he reminded her.

"Right." Now *she* took a deep breath. "Suppose you had to choose between your family and your art. Which one would you keep?"

Chapter Eight

Jess had no idea how Dylan would answer her question.

Evidently, neither did he. She waited, chasing drips on her ice-cream cone, while he finished his, wiped his face and hands and threw the napkin in the trash. He didn't say a word.

Becky and Lizzie reappeared with drinks and giant pretzels in their hands. Thomas and Marcos came up with roasted turkey legs while Nate brought a flavored ice cone that was half blue, half red. Justino and Lena each carried a foot-long sub sandwich and a giant drink. Jess wondered if Lena would consume the whole thing, and how she stayed so thin if she could.

Walking back to their seats, Dylan kept an eye on the kids but didn't volunteer any of his usual quips and comments. Even after they sat down, she could tell his attention was not focused on the ribbon pull, a timed event where kids had to run out and pull the ribbon off a goat's tail to stop the clock.

She'd given him a problem to solve. He remained preoccupied, and spent most of the afternoon with his elbows on his knees and his hands gripped together, staring across the landscape into the distance. Jess noticed the worried glances from his brothers, but didn't spend much sympathy on them. The whole family had been taking Dylan for granted. Someone ought to wake them all up.

She did, however, miss his hand holding hers.

When the saddle bronc event started, his awareness returned to the arena. He looked at her and smiled. "Hi."

"Welcome back."

"Thanks. Now you'll get to watch some serious riding—these high school kids have been practicing for years."

She accepted that he wasn't ready to talk. "Why don't they just go pro?"

"There are rules to protect them. The animals they'll be riding here aren't as big as the ones on the pro circuit, and not as skilled. There's a score for the rider, but also a score for the animal in these events. And sometimes the animal gets hooked on adrenaline just like the human does, and tries its best to get rid of the pesky critter between its shoulder blades."

"Imagine that."

He talked her through the rough stock events, as he called them—saddle bronc, bareback and bull riding. Despite the fact that these animals were smaller and less aggressive, Jess thought the sport seemed too dangerous.

"I can't imagine sitting here and watching my child or my husband get thrown around," she told him as they walked to the barbecue tent for dinner. "Would you let your child compete in a rodeo at those upper levels? As you did?"

Dylan grinned. "Hey, that's another question. I'm not sure I owe you that one." He sobered quickly.

"Look, we're helping these kids learn to ride a bucking animal. The chances that any of them will go on to compete are slim—it's more about the fun and the riding skills at this point. Ford rode bulls in college, Garrett did bareback and I was on saddle broncs. Wyatt's such a big guy, he was into calf roping, and he was a master at it."

"None of which answers the question. Would you let your son or daughter ride a bull?"

When he met her gaze, the pain in his eyes seemed out of proportion to the subject. "If I had a son or a daughter, I would do everything in my power to protect them from ever getting hurt, including rodeo rides." He tried to brighten up. "But then, I've got that artistic taint, you know. You ought to survey the rest of the family, see what they think."

"I might just do that."

After dinner, Jess discovered, there was a rodeo dance. The teenagers from the Circle M were anxious to stay, and once Caroline had reminded them of the rules—no going outside, no going to the bathroom alone, no leaving with anyone whether known or unknown—they were given permission to enjoy themselves. Ford and Caroline joined the dancing right away, and were a pleasure to watch.

"That's called a two-step," Dylan said in her ear. "Want to learn?"

"I'm not much of a dancer…"

"Yet," he said, and grabbed her hands. "Slow, slow, fast-fast." He demonstrated, moving his feet side to side. "That's all there is to it. Slow, slow, fast-fast."

"Slow, slow, fast-fast. That doesn't seem too hard."

They joined the crowd and shuffled around in a circle, saying the words to each other. Occasionally she got confused, and Dylan smiled. For longer and longer stretches, though, she kept going and he grinned. That grin made her feel happier than she could remember ever being before.

Which was a scary experience. But not scary enough to make her stop.

"Okay," he said after their second circle, "we're going to try something new. Just relax, keep doing what you're doing. I'm going to pull a little on this hand and let this one go—keep dancing…"

The next thing she knew, Jess had turned in a circle. "It's a spin! I did a spin!"

"Yep. Do it again."

By the end of the song, she'd also learned to go under his arm and come out again, and they were beginning to look as natural as the other couples.

"This is so much fun," she told him as they walked off the floor holding hands. "I could dance all night."

"Sounds like a song I heard once."

Garrett straightened up from the wall. "You two picked that up fast."

"Jess is a lethal weapon," Dylan explained. "She takes karate. You want to watch that you don't make her mad."

The other Marshall held his hands up. "I'm a man of peace myself. But can I have the next two-step?"

"Of course." Only after she said it did Jess notice the frown on Dylan's face. Maybe she should have asked him. But really, what harm could a dance do?

Garrett led her to a place on the floor with the next appropriate tune. She was still saying "Slow, slow, fast-fast" to herself, but things seemed to be going pretty well.

Then he said, "Dylan mentioned you'll be staying past Sunday to work with the kids on reading and writing."

Jess nodded. "I'm really excited to have this opportunity. I didn't realize how much I would enjoy spending time with teenagers."

"And Dylan, too, I guess."

She lost her place in the pattern and stumbled. "I'm not sure what you mean."

"You two are...involved?"

"Why would you ask? And why would I tell you either way?" And that was assuming she knew the answer, which she did not.

"You will be leaving eventually, right?"

"I have a life in New York." Sort of. "What's your point, Garrett?"

"I'd hate to see my brother hurt because he fell too hard and then had to let go. It might be best to put some distance between the two of you—"

A hand clamped on Garrett's shoulder and jerked him around to face a furious Dylan. "Being a minister— hell, being my brother—does not give you the right to interfere in my life. Back off. Now."

To his credit, Garrett did not seem flustered. "Just looking out for you, Dylan. You're not the best at protecting yourself." He considered Jess as the other couples danced around them. "I didn't mean to insult you. You're a beautiful, intelligent, fascinating woman. But he's my little brother." In the next moment, he was gone.

"Let's dance." Dylan took her in his arms and they

moved into the now-familiar rhythm. "I'm going to punch him one day."

"You haven't yet?" Jess was pretty irritated by the encounter herself. In her opinion, the older Marshall brothers needed some guidance when it came to living with their younger brother.

"Not since I was thirteen. But I think the time might have come around again."

They danced till the music changed, then went to stand against a different wall from the one Garrett was leaning on. Dylan pressed his fingertips against his eyes. "I think the time has also come for this day to be over."

Jess glanced around the dance hall. "Maybe Caroline does, too. Looks like she's rounding up the teenagers. Will there be fireworks before we go? I love fireworks."

Dylan grinned. "Me, too. But the animals don't. No sense causing a panic in the pens."

She hadn't thought of that, of course. "Got it."

The drive home was quiet. Becky and Lizzie both dozed off almost as soon as the truck left the rodeo arena. Even Caroline nodded sleepily in the front passenger seat. Becky leaned against the window glass, snoring slightly. But Lizzie stayed sitting up straight, until Dylan turned a corner and her head fell against Jess's shoulder. The girl didn't wake up, but continued to sleep.

Jess smiled—she'd never had a child sleep on her shoulder before. Or anyone else, that she could remember. Her love affairs, such as they were, hadn't included falling asleep sitting on the couch.

After a long silence, she was surprised when Dylan

spoke out of the darkness. "I didn't answer your question."

She kept her voice low. "I didn't know if you'd decided."

"It took a long time, especially after Garrett staged his intervention at the dance. I was ready to hop on a plane to New York right about then."

"He cares about you. They all do."

"Yeah." He sighed. "And I care about them. Which, when I get down to it, is the answer. I was gone for five years. I came home on purpose and I don't plan to leave again. Ever. If that meant giving up sculpting… I would."

"I hope your brothers realize how much you're prepared to sacrifice for them."

"The Marshall brothers stick together. Ford came back from San Francisco. I'll be here, on the ranch. It's what we do."

Jess pondered his choice for the remainder of the drive. She admired Dylan's dedication to family—what a gift, to have such a fine man so committed to you and your welfare. At the same time, she regretted the artistic talent that would never be given full expression. As long as he remained part of the workforce on the Circle M Ranch, and as long as his brothers continued to take advantage of his willingness to help out whenever he was needed, Dylan wouldn't be free to stretch himself to his full potential. He would only continue the work that fit into his lifestyle, without considering how much more he could accomplish. She would love to see what he could do with those two sketches, the one of Wyatt and the mother and child. But she felt sure he would never push himself on those pieces as long as so much of his energy went to ranch work.

He simply couldn't afford the emotional and physical drain. He was running close to empty as it was.

Wyatt, Susannah and Amber were on the front porch of the house when the truck and the van pulled up. The drowsy teenagers straggled to the bunkhouse and the cabin, except for Nate, who sat down on the porch floor with his little sister in his lap. Wyatt came over to Dylan's truck and opened the door for Caroline, then Jess.

"I wanted to talk to you for a minute," he said. "The sheriff's deputy was out this afternoon. His opinion echoed yours, Dylan. Having the teenagers here practically guaranteed this kind of incident, as far as he was concerned."

Caroline made a growling noise. "Yes, law enforcement is quick to suspect kids, whether or not there's evidence." She glared at Wyatt. "I am willing to bet all the money Jess lost that this was not one of our kids." Then she turned on her heel and walked toward the cabin without waiting for a response.

"I didn't say I agreed with the man." Wyatt heaved a sigh. "I'm tired and I'm going to bed. Good night." His boot heels sounded on the porch as he went inside. Susannah, Amber and Nate had already vanished.

Ford watched his fiancée stalking up the hill. "I think I'll go smooth ruffled feathers. Night."

"I'll check on the boys," Garrett said. He looked at Dylan, and then Jess. With a nod to each of them, he headed toward the bunkhouse.

"Well, that party ended fast." Dylan dropped his head back to gaze at the sky. "Want to go for a walk?"

"In the dark?" But his hand had already found hers. She followed willingly.

When he turned off the path to the red barn, she realized where they were going, and let him lead her down the hill to the creek. Without a mishap or a stumble, Dylan took her straight to the stone they'd sat on before. By that time her eyes had adjusted to the dark and she could detect the silhouettes of the trees, black smudges against the night, and the lighter surfaces of the rocks, the froth of foam in the creek.

They sat side by side, still holding hands. The boulder beneath them radiated the day's warmth. "I hate to go in there," he said, nodding toward the studio. "Not without making things right."

"You could sleep at the house, wait till the morning."

"Yeah. I might do that. That couch is pretty comfortable."

The darkness around them was far from silent—over the rushing water she could hear chirps and burps in every direction. "What makes all the noise?" she asked Dylan.

"Crickets and frogs, cicadas. The usual outdoor chorus."

Jess picked her feet up. "Do they bite?"

"No, silly. Haven't you sat and listened to bugs at night?"

"I've been an urban dweller my entire life. I didn't play outside much."

She drew a quick breath as the pad of his thumb stroked along her jawline. "No wonder your skin is so fine. You haven't let the sun get to it." He stroked again. "You don't even need makeup. Those freckles across your nose are lovely."

"People expect the mask." His fingers curved around the nape of her neck and lifted her hair up off her shoulders. "That feels wonderful. It gets heavy sometimes."

"I bet." His fingers threaded through the length. "You could keep it shorter. You'd still be gorgeous."

"Then I'd have to change my profile picture. And longer hair makes you look younger, if you keep it styled."

"So many rules in your business." Strong fingers massaged her left shoulder, and then her right. "You must stay tense."

Jess shivered. "You're taking care of it."

"Glad I can help." She relaxed as his arm circled her back, with his hand resting at her waist. "See how I did that? Pretty smooth, hmm?" His lips touched her temple. "I love your perfume. Thank God for Coco Chanel."

She actually giggled. "You've got a pretty sexy scent, yourself."

His other hand came up to her cheek and turned her face toward him. "At least I don't smell like a horse tonight."

Before she could laugh, he bent his head and swept her into a kiss. She wasn't surprised, but she gave a small gasp, because his mouth felt so wonderful joined with hers.

Dylan chuckled. "It's amazing," he said, his breath whispering over her lips, "how good we are together."

"Dylan..." She tried to be sane. "This isn't a smart idea..."

"You're my diversion," he murmured. "Keeping my mind off my troubles."

Jess understood that reasoning all too well. The night had turned fluid, a swirling darkness where the anchor was his shoulder under her palm and their mouths locked together, moving, sliding, clinging as they created an intensity of pleasure she'd never known. Her hand on the back of his neck discovered the smoothness of his skin and the crisp waves of his hair. She explored further and found the sleek muscles of his upper arm under the crisp cotton shirt, the light dusting of hair on his bare forearm.

"It's not fair," she told him as he skimmed his mouth over her chin and along the curve of her throat.

"What's that?"

"You've got two arms around me, but I can only use one."

"Simple to solve." In the next moment, he eased her down, until they were lying side by side on the boulder. "Better?"

She circled both her arms around his shoulders. "Much."

He groaned as she ran her hands up and down his back. "Oh, yes."

For all Jess noticed, the stone beneath them might have been a feather bed. She was consumed in Dylan, stroking her hands over the long lines of his body, the firm muscles and smooth skin under his shirt. He kept an arm under her head, but his other hand managed to be everywhere—her breasts, her thighs, her belly and, tenderly, her face.

"Beautiful," he said, pressing his kisses against her breastbone. "You are so beautiful." He raised his head to meet her eyes, a glint of laughter in his own. "Your soul is beautiful, too. I wouldn't want you to think I'm a superficial guy."

"Superficial has its useful moments." She skimmed her hands along his ribs. "Carry on."

Dylan fingered the neck of her T-shirt, and Jess gasped when he slipped his hand inside to graze his knuckles against the tops of her breasts. "I would undress you right here under the stars, but with our luck, a teenager would come wandering down the hill for the first time since they've been here. That's the kind of day it's been."

He helped her sit up again, then got to his feet and held out a hand. "We can go to the studio. Or…" She heard his deep breath. "I can walk you to the house. Your choice."

The moon hadn't risen, so he was a form in the dark, a cowboy-shaped shadow. And she wanted him.

The rules she'd set for herself raced through her mind.

Taking his hand, Jess stood up beside him. Then she turned and led him across the grass toward the blue door.

DYLAN OPENED THE studio door but didn't turn on the overhead lights, leading Jess around the tables using only the glow from a single lamp by the bed in the loft. Atmosphere mattered to women. After starting this seduction on a rock, he figured he could make at least a little more effort.

And he refused to think about the catastrophe in his studio.

"Would you like some wine?" he asked as they

climbed the steps still hand in hand. "Or a drink? I have whiskey, coffee and iced tea. Take your pick."

"You," she said at the top. When he turned to look at her, she pushed at his chest, walking him backward until the bed hit his calves. "Just you."

Grinning, he allowed her to push him until he fell onto the mattress. Jess came down on top of him, with her knees on either side of his hips.

"Just." She kissed him, and then started on the buttons of his shirt. "You."

The night went wild. By the time she got his shirt unbuttoned, he had pulled her T-shirt over her head and thrown it away.

Then he groaned. "I'm glad I didn't know what you wore underneath that black shirt. It would have made me crazy all day." She was sexy as hell in a red, low-cut bra. "Does the bottom match?"

She gave him a wicked smile. "Maybe."

Dylan groaned again. "I'm dying, here." He went for the buckle on her belt and then the snap on her jeans. Just a short slide of the zipper proved the truth.

Velvet skin and red silk lingerie sent him over the edge. He wanted to touch, to taste every inch of her, and he made the supreme effort. She countered him with moves of her own, kisses and nips in unexpected places, her palms sliding intimately across his flesh, her wicked whispers making him that much hotter. He didn't believe he could last a second longer, and yet he held back, not wanting the most incredible experience of his life to end. Sex had never been this good before. Would never be this good again with anyone but Jess.

Suddenly she was underneath him in the way he'd fantasized, naked and eager, her big golden eyes pleading with him to give them both the climax they craved. With their bodies joined, Dylan began to move, slowly, carefully at first, but then faster and stronger until he lost control and the two of them reached the firmament together.

Afterward, he managed not to fall on top of Jess, but to the side. It took a while for him to catch enough breath to speak. "You okay?"

"I'm wonderful." Head on his shoulder, she curled against his side like a contented cat. "You?"

"Perfect." He kissed her forehead. "Or as close as I'll ever get."

A laugh shook her. Then, between one breath and the next, Jess Granger fell asleep.

Dylan chuckled. Without disturbing her, he reached down to the foot of the bed and grabbed the blanket, covered both of them with it, and then he let his eyes close, too.

He woke her sometime in the night to make love again, more slowly but with even more intensity. The next time he opened his eyes, dawn was lighting the windows and Jess was coming up the stairs with two cups of coffee. She wore her black T-shirt, which almost reached to the top of those red panties.

"I'm pretty sure I don't need another stimulant," he said as she handed him a mug. "You're quite enough, thanks." He bent his knees to tent the blanket and conceal his body's predictable response to...well, to everything about Jess Granger.

She toasted him with her cup. "I should probably have sneaked back into the house under cover of darkness. Garrett will be in the kitchen by now."

"Garrett's long gone. It's Sunday, so he goes to the

church in town early to review his sermon and make sure everything is ready for services."

"In that case…" She set her cup on the bedside table and threw herself on the bed beside him. "We could get more sleep. Or something."

He put his cup down and let himself fall into her kisses for a few minutes, then pulled back slightly. "I am supposed to be feeding the horses in about twenty minutes."

Jess joined him under the covers and put her warm palms on his bare chest. "That's plenty of time."

Dylan was only a little late to feed the horses, but he found Ford there ahead of him, putting grain in buckets. "Good morning," his brother said evenly, without pausing in his task.

"Yes, it is. I'll take those out to the field." He whistled as he waited.

"You're in a fine mood for so early."

"Sometimes you just wake up that way."

Ford cleared his throat. "Your private life is your business—"

"Thanks, that's all you should say." Dylan stepped over to pick up the stacked buckets.

"But she *will* leave."

"I'll deal with that when it happens."

"We need you functional."

He rolled his eyes. "What am I, fifteen? I've dealt with much worse in life than being dumped. I can handle my own relationships without falling apart. Though God forbid anybody but Wyatt require a respite. The whole place would fall to pieces." He walked across the corral toward the pasture gate, no longer whistling. His mood didn't matter to the horses, who were all stationed at their usual tubs, waiting for breakfast.

His brothers couldn't seem to leave it alone. When he went into the house, Jess was nowhere to be seen but Wyatt was seated at the dining room table with his coffee, obviously waiting. The door to the kitchen was closed.

"Got a minute?" he asked, but his tone didn't invite a refusal.

So Dylan sat down. "Could we skip the lecture? Consider it said?"

"Sure. Can we assume you'll keep your relationship out of sight so the kids won't get the impression that this is approved behavior?"

"What's not to approve? Wait, I know." He held up a hand. "Only within the bonds of holy matrimony. Could I just point out you don't seem to have a problem with Ford and Caroline spending the night in town together?"

"They're engaged. And they're not on the ranch. Playing games under the teenagers' noses is asking for the same kind of behavior from them."

"Yes, Wyatt, we will be discreet. Yes, Ford," who had just walked into the room, "I'll keep my chores done even when Jess has to return to New York." He hadn't said it aloud before that moment. Maybe he hadn't quite believed it would happen. "And I'll try to be sure my 'hobby' doesn't interfere with anybody else's life." He pushed the chair back and stood. "Anything else?"

At that moment, Susannah pushed the kitchen door open. She carried a plate in one hand and a coffee mug in the other. "Hi, Dylan. I thought you might want to eat in here instead of the kitchen."

He shook his head. "Thanks, but I'm not hungry. I'll be in the studio cleaning up, if somebody needs me." Brushing by Ford, he left the house with a slam of the screen door.

When he reached the bottom of his hill, instead of going into the studio he walked down to the creek and sat on the boulder he thought of as his. Or, now, *theirs*. Memories of the moments they'd lain there seemed to drift over him like falling petals on the morning breeze.

He didn't regret what he'd done. How could anyone regret such a wondrous experience? He'd be content to spend the rest of his life waking up with Jess Granger in his arms.

But, as his brothers had so kindly pointed out, that was the problem. Jess wouldn't stay. He couldn't imagine why she would make that choice, even if she had fallen in love with him in a matter of four days. And that wasn't at all realistic, even if he'd fallen in love with her.

Why else would he make love to her? He hadn't changed his mind about casual sex, or commitment. His brothers thought they were so smart, trying to warn him off from getting too involved—they didn't see that he was already too involved, had been since Thursday afternoon, when he'd listened to her talk about her past and realized what a strong and dependable person she must be. A woman who could build a successful life with absolutely no one's help would be a partner he wanted to make a home and family with. He would trust her with his life. More important, he would trust her with the lives of his children.

But there was no reason to think Jess had fallen in love with him. She didn't want to need people—he understood that. And he had no idea how he could convince her that relationships could be permanent, could last an entire lifetime.

Dylan laughed at himself. He wasn't sure how he knew relationships could last a lifetime. He'd never had a romance last six months.

Except that Wyatt had been there for him every day of his twenty-seven years. Ford and Garrett, too, even if they ticked him off. If he cast his mind further afield, he could think of others who had demonstrated that kind of loyalty to him. Mr. and Mrs. Harris had celebrated their fortieth anniversary last fall. Several couples in Garrett's church had seen their fiftieth. Hell, Kip Glazier had been his friend since fifth grade. Seventeen years was a long time.

But just promising Jess forever would mean nothing. And how would he show her, except day by day? He didn't have much to offer to keep her in Wyoming. Nothing she valued, anyway, such as laundries and Chinese takeout, fancy ice cream, a good job and a place of her own without his brothers watching her every move. And not just because she was such a pleasure to watch when she walked.

He would have to accept the idea that she would go. She hadn't mentioned how much longer she'd stay, but a week would be pushing it. She'd probably need more clothes, if nothing else.

And so he would enjoy this week, treasuring every moment they were together. Even when they weren't alone, he'd value the time he could watch her, talk with her, learn from her. When they were alone, he would make those moments a sensual and satisfying experience. And when the day came when Jess had to leave, he would watch her walk away with his pride intact, if not his heart.

But then, an artist could do great work with a broken heart.

"Here again?"

There she was, looking more gorgeous than ever. "Yeah... I wasn't quite ready to tackle the cleanup."

"I wasn't sure what was going on. You said something about church..."

"We haven't been making the kids go—didn't want to offend anybody's parents. Garrett does a...what's he call it?...a homily, right after lunch. Sunday morning is sleep-in day for the kids."

She sat beside him, but not close enough that they were touching. "Your house isn't well soundproofed."

"I figured you would hear the conversation."

"I could leave—"

He put his hand over hers, clasped in her lap. "No. You wanted to work with the kids this week. You should have that chance. And I want you to stay. If that matters."

"Of course it does. I just hate making trouble with your brothers."

"You won't be the first girl who did."

"Or the last?"

An interesting question, coming from Jess. "I'm getting pretty old. My troublemaking days may be over."

"Ancient," she teased. "I noticed last night how weak you are."

"Yeah, I'm sorry about that."

Jess stood up and drew him with her. "Susannah had me bring your breakfast over here. Come have something to eat. In just four days, I know you're always starving."

"Must be your nose for news."

"A man's appetite isn't news. Just a fact of life."

"Wisdom and beauty, all in one package."

"Are you ever serious? Do you ever give a straight answer?"

Dylan opened the door to the studio. "I'm thinking about it."

JESS HAD BROUGHT the computer Ford had loaned her, but first she helped Dylan put the studio to rights. Of the three pieces set on fire, only one had been seriously burned, the eagle in flight, but the damage was mostly scorching and not actual destruction.

"Kind of interesting," Dylan commented as he examined it. "Like the story of Icarus, who flew too close to the sun with wings made of wax. The eagle flies too close and his wings are scorched."

"Or else it's a comment on the quality of our environment—the lives of eagles are threatened by what's happening with pollution."

He nodded. "That, too. Maybe I should incorporate scorching as a technique. I'm always willing to learn new tricks." Glancing around the studio, his face relaxed from the tension he'd worn for the past twenty-four hours. "This is better. I can handle the rest of the work. You're relieved of cleanup duty."

Relieved that Dylan was feeling in control again, Jess opened the computer and started putting together the article she needed to write. Having the subject right there to verify facts and quotes was a luxury she didn't usually enjoy.

On the other hand, telling this particular story without having all the information proved quite a challenge. She had checked her research of the women he'd dated while in the limelight, but no one stood out as a potential heartbreaker. Noelle Kristenson had been his last girlfriend mentioned in the gossip columns. But she'd remained prominent on the social scene after Dylan left. Jess couldn't establish any kind of connection between his abrupt departure and their relationship.

Unless she asked. "Do you remember Noelle Kristenson?"

"Um...sure. Pretty lady." He didn't look up from his sweeping.

"You dated her."

"I did."

"Right before you came home."

"If you say so."

"Did she have anything to do with why you left?"

He was quiet for a full minute. "Yes."

Finally. "You had a fight?"

"Yes."

"You were so in love with her?"

"No!" He rubbed his hands over his face. "No, I didn't love Noelle. But what she did—I couldn't deal with it."

"What did she do?"

This silence lasted much longer, as he stood motionless with the broom. "Most men probably wouldn't care. It's a choice, right?"

"Dylan, what happened?"

"Noelle got pregnant." He pulled in a deep breath. "She didn't tell me. Until after she'd had an abortion."

Chapter Nine

"She wouldn't surrender her lifestyle," he continued. "Not even for nine months. I would have taken the baby to raise, but she didn't give me the chance." Raw pain roughened his voice.

"That's terrible." Jess immediately thought of the drawing of mother and baby he kept above his drawing table. Now she knew who the artist had been. "Children are so important to you."

"They should matter to everyone. And I kept thinking that my parents could have made the same choice. They had three sons and not much money. Mom was already sick. They could have eased the load." He lifted his chin to meet her eyes. "What if your mother had made the same decision? Would you trade your life, hard as it's been, for…nothing?"

"Of course not. Life is always worth living."

Dylan nodded. Then he walked over to a window, standing with his back to her. "The worst part—the despicable, shameful part—is that when she told me, for just a second… I was relieved." After a pause, he said, "I hate myself for that."

"You're human."

His shoulders rose on a deep breath, and he turned

to face her. "So there you have it, Ms. Granger. My deep, dark secret. I went to see my piece in the sculpture garden in Paris that afternoon and I didn't recognize anything about it as belonging to me. I couldn't imagine how I'd ever believed that kind of work meant something. And I realized I didn't want to be the person I'd become, who could dispose of a child as easily—more easily!—than a hunk of concrete and iron. So I caught the first flight out and came home." He held his hands out from his sides. "End of story."

Jess watched from across the room as he faced the window again. She had the truth now. With such great material, the article would write itself. Her editor would be thrilled with this kind of sexy, emotional twist. She wouldn't use Noelle's name, of course. Her job would be to protect the woman, while exposing Dylan to public scrutiny.

"Why reveal this to me now?" she asked him. "Why put such a weapon in my hands?" Then she had an insight. "Your brothers don't know what happened, do they?"

"No. I wouldn't give them the pain. I'm telling you because I love you. I want you to have the truth about me."

"Dylan—" Her heart thundered in her chest. "You can't fall in love in four days."

"Maybe *you* can't. But I did." His grin was a ghost of its usual self. "I'm not expecting anything, Jess. I understand you've got a life you intend to return to. I'll enjoy you while you're here, and when you go, I'll have some great memories. Don't worry—I won't be maudlin about it. That's not my style."

"No." She couldn't catch her breath. Her hands

were cold and her face blazing hot. Maybe she would pass out. Shock did that to people.

Dylan didn't come across the room and attempt to persuade her. "I'm going to take Leo out for a ride," he said instead. "Give you some breathing room. I'll be gone a couple of hours." He picked up his hat from the table and waved briefly before letting himself out the blue door.

Jess put her head down on her arms. This was worse than waking up in his bed that first morning. Today she'd woken up to find herself in his heart.

And it would be so terribly easy to stay there. So comfortable to let herself love him in return.

In fact, despite what she'd told him, she already did. She'd loved him under the stars by the creek, and all during the passionate storm they'd raised in each other throughout the night. She'd loved him on his knees in the dust beside a fallen Lizzie, and riding off across the field on Leo's bare back. As hard as she'd fought not to, Jess might have loved Dylan Marshall from the moment she saw him, not quite five days ago.

But he could never find out. The worst thing she could do for Dylan would be to confess that she loved him, too. He would want to build a future for the two of them, together.

And Jess was certain that she was the last woman Dylan Marshall should marry.

With her back aching from the uncomfortable chair, she got up and walked around the studio, hardly noticing all the exquisite sculptures she passed. She ended up, as she'd probably subconsciously intended, at the drawing table and the beautiful sketch above it. If she had to bet, she would wager a month's pay that the drawing had been done by Dylan's mother, capturing a moment between them when he was an infant. Something about those wide dark eyes had always reminded her of him.

The vandal had taken some of the drawings from the table and used them to set the fire. But the trash can, pushed inside the kneehole of the desk, had escaped his notice. On a hunch, Jess crouched over the container and fingered through the pages, curious to see what Dylan had thrown away. Most of the sketches were of sculptures he had already shown her.

But he'd thrown away the two drawings of people— his copy of his mother's picture and the bust he'd done of Wyatt. At least he hadn't crumpled them up. Jess pulled them out of the trash still smooth, with only a single crease in the center.

Why would he discard work with such potential? Why wasn't he dying to translate these images into solid form? What kept him blocked?

Taking the sheets to the table where she'd been working, Jess slipped them behind some pages in her notebook. She wasn't sure if she wanted them for Dylan or for herself. But she couldn't let them disappear.

Then she sat down at the table again and pulled the computer in front of her. She had a challenging task ahead—to salvage Dylan's current career, restore his reputation and somehow convincingly relate his story without ever hinting at the truth.

WHEN DYLAN BROUGHT LEO back to the barn after their ride, the kids were out and about, hanging around in the general vicinity. As soon as he got off they started gathering around him—they all seemed to love his flashy, spotted horse, and Leo was a sucker for being spoiled, so the combination worked out well. Even Thomas and Marcos liked taking Leo to the wash stall for a rinse, drying him off and combing out his mane and tail. Becky and Nate, the real horse lovers, cleaned the horse's feet and fed him treats while Lena and Justino used the gathering as an excuse to be together. Today, there didn't seem to be as much comfortable chatter as usual, but the past days had been busy with the cattle drive and the rodeo. Everybody might just be tired. Dylan knew he was.

Lizzie, he noted also, didn't participate. She sat on a hay bale at the front of the barn, playing a game on her phone. She'd never been comfortable with any horse except Major, and now that trust had been broken, which set her apart from the rest of the group.

Dylan walked over and leaned on the wall next to her. "Having a nice day?"

She shrugged a thin shoulder. "It's okay."

"I have to say, I'm very impressed that you're a writer."

"I'm not a writer. I just write stuff down that I make up."

"As far as I'm concerned, that qualifies you as an official writer. I write when I have to, but I've never been good at it."

"But you make sculptures. And you can draw. You're an artist."

That wasn't the direction he wanted to take with the conversation. "Yes. We're all born with certain talents, I guess, or maybe certain ways we choose to express ourselves. I couldn't write a poem in a month of Sundays."

"But you can ride a horse."

That was the opening he wanted. "So can you."

"I wasn't born wanting to ride."

"Funny thing, neither was I."

She frowned up at him. "You weren't? I thought all of you started being cowboys when you were little."

"Nope. Wyatt was sixteen when he rode his first horse. I was eleven. We lived in town and never even saw horses, except from a distance, until then."

"Did you fall off?"

"I've probably fallen off a hundred times, and that doesn't even include when I was learning to ride bucking broncs. We all fall off. The trick is to get back on."

Lizzie shook her head. "I was so scared those cows would run right over me."

"That didn't happen, did it? Major kept you out of the way." He crouched down in front of her to look into her face. "I have a trick we could work on, just you and me. I think it would help you stay on. It's the way I learned."

She eyed him with suspicion. "What is it?"

"Can you trust me? We'll go try it out right this minute, while everybody is busy."

"Will I get hurt?"

"Absolutely not."

"Okay." She followed him down the aisle to pick up a halter and a helmet, then across the corral to the pasture fence.

"Major's right there, waiting for us," Dylan pointed out, and went to bring the pony in. "Now we're going over to the mounting block." Once there, he positioned Major beside it. "All I want you to do, Lizzie, is get on."

"There's no saddle!"

"That's right. I want you to get on his bare back."

She retreated almost to the fence. "I can't do that. I'll slide right off."

"No, you won't, because you can hold on..." He grabbed a handful of Major's black mane. "Right here. He's got a nice flat spine and a good solid handle attached to his neck. You won't fall."

Dylan waited through her indecision. He figured she hated being the only one who wouldn't ride. Facing the coming week isolated from her companions couldn't be a pleasant prospect.

Finally, she took a step forward, and another. She got to the mounting block and stood on the top. "Now what? Where do I put my feet?"

"He's going to stand real still. Bend over and grab some of his mane with both hands and hold on tight. Then just swing your leg over, like you would with a saddle, and sit down."

Lizzie took a deep breath, grabbed Major's mane and then threw her leg about halfway over.

"Keep going," Dylan told her quietly. "That leg's gotta hang off the other side."

With the next try, Lizzie ended sitting on Major's back, hunched over close to the pony's neck.

"Straighten up," he instructed her. "Let your legs stretch all the way to the ground."

"They won't do that."

"Pretend they will. It'll help you keep your balance." She pushed her heels down. "That's exactly right. So now keep those legs stretched and those hands in his mane. We're going to go for a slooooow walk."

She squeaked as Major took his first couple of steps, and she wobbled a little. But the pony did have a flat back and a smooth gait, so in a matter of minutes, the girl started to adjust. Dylan didn't say much, just an encouraging comment here and there as he led Major slowly around the corral, changing directions occasionally, going in straight lines and circles, as Lizzie rode.

When they came to a stop, he grinned at her. "Look at you—a bareback rider! How does it feel?"

Being fourteen and "cool," she couldn't admit how much she'd enjoyed the experience. "Okay, I guess. But how do I get down?"

"Pretty much the same way. Lean forward, bring your right leg over and slide off."

She practically bounced when her feet hit the ground. "Wow. That was…" She glanced at Dylan and away again. "Pretty good."

"I'm glad you think so. We can do some more work, getting you better balanced and more comfortable out of the saddle. Then getting into the saddle again will be easy." He stepped close and bent to whisper in her ear. "Hey, Lizzie. You got back on the horse. You're a rider."

Despite herself, she grinned. "I am, aren't I?"

JESS STOOD IN the barn, watching as Dylan and Lizzie high-fived each other out in the corral. She'd been planning on talking to one or more of the teenagers about their writing this afternoon, but had found them all occupied with Dylan's horse. And then she'd watched the man himself rehabilitate Lizzie, teaching her to ride without a saddle, of all things.

His brothers didn't even realize what an asset they had in their little brother. Of course, they'd probably take the credit for having been the ones who brought him up. But Jess thought Dylan's best qualities— caring, commitment and honesty—were choices he'd made for himself. He wasn't simply a product of his environment and his family. He'd deliberately decided what kind of man he intended to become and then arranged his life accordingly. She could only admire that determination.

Even if she couldn't share that life.

Lizzie didn't see her in the doorway as she slipped out the side gate of the corral. While watching Dylan lead the pony back to the pasture, Jess became aware that a squabble had broken out between the kids working on Leo. Well, two of the kids, anyway.

"I'm walkin' him out," Marcos said. "It's my turn."

"Who says?" Thomas had a snarl in his voice. "Nate did it last time. I haven't done it. It's my turn."

"Come on, guys." Becky sounded almost like one of the adults. "Do you have to argue about everything?" Justino and Lena sat on a nearby bench, absorbed in one another and their phones.

"When somebody takes advantage," Thomas growled, "then, yeah, you have to argue."

Jess walked through the barn until she found the big concrete-floored stall where they had rinsed the horse. "I'm not an expert, but angry voices don't seem like the right choice when you want the animal you're working with to stay calm. Maybe you guys should chill out."

The two boys glared at each other across Leo's back. Meanwhile, Becky untied the horse and walked it between them. "I'll take him to the pasture. I haven't done it, either." She grinned at Jess as she passed.

The anger level hadn't receded much. Jess thought fast. "Thomas, I wondered if we could talk about your writing and reading this afternoon. I'm really interested to hear how you're enjoying the book you chose. Would now be a good time?"

"Do I have to?"

Jess couldn't say yes, but she stared him down.

"Okay." He headed toward the exit.

"We have to clean the place up," Marcos yelled after him. "I'm not doin' it by myself."

"I'll do it," Nate said quietly, from the rear corner of the stall. "Just go on."

"Hey, man. That's great." In the next instant, Marcos had disappeared.

"Sorry," Jess told the boy. "Do you want some help?"

He smiled, and suddenly he looked like his mother. "I enjoy doing it without them. It's a lot more fun without all the complaining."

She laughed with him, and went to find Thomas, hoping this session wouldn't be the struggle she anticipated. He had waited for her at the dining table in the bunkhouse, as sullen as a student sentenced to stay after school for bad behavior. Jess recognized the demeanor, having often been one of those kids herself.

"Thanks for meeting with me," she said as she sat across the table from him. "I appreciated what you had to say in the paragraph you wrote. And you write very well."

His dark gaze was cool as it met hers. "Just because I'm Indian doesn't mean I can't speak and write the English language."

"That's true. You have a strong sense of the injustice that's been done to Native Americans."

"That happens when you live on the rez. You get to see how far a treaty goes."

"What do you think of *The Last of the Mohicans*?"

"Kinda slow."

"It was written almost two hundred years ago."

"Yeah. But what happens in the story is interesting. A lousy ending, though."

"You've read the entire book?"

He shook his head. "No, but when you put Indians and whites together, the ending is always bad for the red man."

PEACE REIGNED ON the ranch that evening, as kids and adults gathered in the living room. Wyatt had started a nice blaze in the fireplace and Susannah brought out the makings for a treat involving marshmallows, chocolate bars and graham crackers.

"They're called s'mores," Dylan informed Jess when she asked. "You roast the marshmallow, then close it with a chocolate bar between two graham crackers. Here." He gave her a skewer with a marshmallow on it. "Take this to the fire and get it nice and brown."

Before she could decide it was brown enough, though, the marshmallow caught on fire. "Dylan! Help!"

The kids around her were laughing as he came to the rescue. "That's perfect." He blew the fire out. "Get your crackers and chocolate ready. Now…" He laid the marshmallow down on the chocolate bar. "Squeeze them together. That's right." The skewer slid out from the chocolate-marshmallow goo. "You're good to go."

Jess tried a bite, ending up with chocolate dripping down her chin. "That is…oh, gosh…amazing. So delicious." She finished the whole sandwich and licked her fingers. "You people sure know how to eat."

"Yes, we do." All the kids went back for a second treat but Jess shook her head when Dylan offered the ingredients. "My clothes aren't going to fit me to wear them home," she protested. "At this rate, I'll have to borrow a trash bag."

She saw his smile dim at the words and realized she'd hurt him. But he would be better off remembering that she wouldn't be here for long, that their time together was temporary. Surely that would be best for both of them.

Susannah brought out coffee for the adults and hot chocolate for the kids, and then Ford took a guitar out of its case and began to strum.

She'd had no idea the Marshalls boasted musical talent, too. But throughout the evening, she heard Ford play all types of tunes—rock, folk, country and even rap. Dylan and Caroline both had good voices, and they harmonized on many of the songs Ford played.

The kids had their own favorites, from silly camp songs such as "On Top of Spaghetti" and "Row, Row, Row Your Boat"—that one, at least, Jess had heard of—to more popular songs from the pop and rap styles. Becky and Lizzie sang a song together, and Thomas and Marcos mugged their way through several more. Nate sat in the corner with Amber, who soon fell asleep in his lap in the dark. Justino and Lena, of course, were glued side by side with their phones in their hands. But even they swayed to the beat and sang a chorus or two.

For the most part Jess watched, and marveled at the circumstances that had brought all these different souls together. Caroline and Garrett had made the plan, but it would never have become a reality without Wyatt's strong determination to be a force for good in his community. Ford and Dylan might have opposed the idea to begin with, but no one could deny their contributions to the welfare of these kids.

And the kids themselves deserved credit for taking the risk to be here in the first place. Jess wasn't sure she would have accepted such an opportunity—the chances of looking bad in front of her peers would have been far too high. Especially at their age.

But then, she'd never opened herself up to a challenging relationship. Not after Trini. And not after her parents, those never-to-be-depended-upon adults in her life. Jess could recognize that she'd deliberately cut herself off from people who might get too close, ask too much of her without giving anything in return.

So how could she ever expect to fit in here? Caroline was obviously a woman for whom giving came naturally. Susannah, too—her care of her children demonstrated her emotional involvement. Garrett, as a minister, had made giving and caring his life's work. Wyatt had kept his family together and raised three younger brothers on his own. That level of self-sacrifice was beyond anything Jess had experienced.

And Dylan...well, Dylan never seemed to think

of himself first, but was always trying to meet the needs and expectations of someone else. He had said to her that he would give up his art career before he would give up his family. That was why he squeezed his sculpture into the time left over at the end of the day, rather than making a perfectly reasonable demand that he be allowed to pursue the career he loved for part of the normal schedule. He ran himself ragged rather than impose his artistic drive on his brothers.

What made his efforts possible were his innate easy-going nature and the abiding love he offered to his family...that he'd offered to her. She'd never met a man so open, so willing to please. None of his brothers could match Dylan for unselfishness—each of them had managed to pursue his own agenda, often at Dylan's expense.

But Jess would admit she was biased. She wanted Dylan to have whatever made him happy. Whatever brought him pleasure, joy, contentment, satisfaction— all the blessings in life—she wanted for Dylan Marshall.

Which was why she had to go. As the kids sang songs around her and the adults smiled at each other and at her, Jess knew she needed to leave the Circle M Ranch as soon as she could. The longer she stayed, the more difficult she would find it to do the right thing.

And doing the right thing was the only way she could help Dylan now.

By the time Ford's voice had gotten hoarse and the kids had eaten all the s'mores they could hold, Jess had gathered her resolve and planned her getaway. She'd even slipped out of the room for a few minutes and made a plane reservation on the computer. Wednesday, she would fly back to New York with a heart full of regrets. But at least spoiling Dylan's life wouldn't be one of them.

Walking to the studio after the kids had gone to bed, she recounted Thomas's comment about white men and red men to Dylan, who laughed loud and long. "A smart kid. He should become a politician—he's already got the sound-bite technique mastered."

"*If* he straightens out his life," Jess said. "He's got quite a temper—one look from Marcos can set him off like a match to dynamite."

"They're friends one minute, enemies the next. We could probably use a counselor out here to work with them. Caroline's trained in direct casework and sociology, not clinical treatment."

"With all the positive intentions you and your brothers have demonstrated, surely these kids have gained a sense that the world can be a better place. I can't help but believe I could have had a much easier adolescence with such decent people on my side."

He took her hand. "You succeeded on your own. That's something to be proud of."

"But—" She wasn't quite sure how to say what she wanted to him to know. "I would be different, I think."

"I don't know of anyone who would want you to be different. Certainly not me." He raised the hand he was holding to kiss the backs of her fingers.

"Oh, no? Wouldn't you want me to be more open, more approachable? Someone friendly and sociable, not wary and reserved?"

He shook his head. "You're not being fair to yourself."

"Someone who likes big parties and big families, who's comfortable in a crowd with lots of kids running around?"

"Jess." He gave her hand a shake. "I love what you are. That's all."

She blinked to clear the tears from her eyes. "You want a family, Dylan. Children love you and you love them in return. You complain about the teenagers, but then you take time to help them with their problems, their fears and concerns. You *need* a family of your own to care for. And I...I couldn't give you that."

"What do you mean?"

"When I was twenty-five, I had to undergo a hysterectomy because of fibroid tumors. They were benign. But...I can't have children."

His face lost its color. "God, Jess. I'm so sorry."

She shrugged. "I didn't expect to have kids. I don't know anything about them, or how to be a parent. I wouldn't let my foster parents close enough. Anyway..." She turned away and stood up out of her chair. "More of me blurting out my history. Sorry about that. I'm going to go up to the house, leave you to get some work done."

Dylan caught her hand again. "Don't go." The tone in his voice conveyed his intentions more clearly than words.

Jess looked back at him. "There's no future for us, Dylan. No sense in getting more involved."

He got to his feet. "I love you. I want as much of your time as I can have, for as long as it lasts."

"You deserve so much more."

Then he kissed her, and put his arms around her. She couldn't think of what was wise or smart or good.

Only that she wanted him as much as he wanted her. That she loved him, too, as much and as deeply as she understood the meaning of the word.

But at least she hadn't told him so.

Chapter Ten

Dylan awoke on Monday morning to the sound of rain on the tin roof of the studio and a view of dripping eaves through the window. He was sorely tempted to burrow under the covers with Jess and sleep for another couple of hours, wake her up with some slow, easy loving, and then amble over to the house, with his arm around her shoulders, for one of Susannah's gigantic breakfasts.

But there were several aspects of that program his brothers would object to, the first being that the horses hadn't been fed. That whole amble idea, once the kids were awake, wouldn't go over too well, either.

So he pushed himself out of bed, showered and dressed, then left a note for Jess saying he'd meet her for breakfast after his chores were done. She smiled in her sleep when he dropped a kiss on her forehead— the second-best way to start his day.

Between feeding in the rain, setting up the tack room for the kids to use when they cleaned their saddles and bridles, sweeping out the barn and brushing down some cobwebs from the ceiling, he didn't get into the house until close to ten o'clock.

Jess was waiting for him in the living room. "I told

Susannah you were coming. She's making your breakfast. But I wanted to talk to you first."

"Sure." He waited till she sat on the couch and took the cushion next to her. "What's going on?"

"I called Patricia Trevor in New York, mentioned I was finishing up the article and just wanted to get her slant on the show and your current approach. I can't believe what she had to say."

"What was it?"

"First, she didn't really remember what kind of work you were doing now and asked me to describe it."

"Well, that's a kick in the ego. I've sold a few pieces here and there, and she said she'd seen one, which was why she called in the first place."

"Then she said that what you were doing sounded rather 'pedestrian,' but that it didn't matter."

"Didn't matter?"

"Because she believes your name alone will draw people to the show. Her main objective is to showcase the Denver gallery itself, and the best way, she decided, was to bring in a crowd. People would meet her, she could make contacts and they'd remember her when they were shopping for real art."

"'Real.' Okay." He blew out a breath. "But why me? I haven't shown in two years."

"She said she wanted to use the notorious—her word—aspect of your reputation. The unsolved mystery of your disappearance. And she figured you and your agent would be desperate and wouldn't ask for as much money as someone who'd exhibited more recently."

"Can't say she's wrong there. My agent was all over this offer." Dylan fell back against the sofa. "Anything else to add to the debacle?"

"As far as the article was concerned, she wanted as much dirt—again, her word—as possible. 'Anything to make noise,' she said. 'The more salacious, the better.'" Jess had tears in her eyes. "I'm sorry, Dylan. I informed her she'd probably be disappointed in the article and hung up before I started swearing at her. I figured you'd want to know."

He linked his fingers with hers and squeezed her hand. "I'm not surprised at Ms. Trevor's attitude, just that she'd be so honest about it. But here's what I think." He stood up and pulled Jess to her feet. "With such low expectations, how can I lose? People will see my work, they'll like it or they won't, they buy or they don't. But I'll have had national exposure in your magazine and a fancy gallery showing. If she can use me, I can use her, too."

"Good point. And you could do some advertising on your own behalf, in magazines aimed at Western art collectors."

"Exactly. You probably have an idea of which ones would be useful. Or can figure it out for me."

"Of course." She threw her arms around his neck for a hug. "You're right—proactive is so much more productive. We could plan an advertising campaign to get the right kind of people into the gallery that night."

Susannah appeared in the doorway to the dining room. "Breakfast is ready. Hope you two are starved. I got a little carried away."

"So are we," Dylan said, grinning. "But isn't it a great feeling?"

BREAKFAST TURNED OUT to be the high point of the day. Jess and Dylan spent a couple of hours researching magazines that would be receptive to advertisements, but when she went to get her camera to take photographs of his work, she realized for the first time that it, too, had been stolen.

"I can't believe I didn't think of it," she said. The memory card with all the shots she'd taken since she'd arrived was in the camera. "I hadn't saved those photos online yet. I've been too busy."

"I'm so sorry." Dylan stood at the door to her room. "It's hard to understand why something can't be done. There aren't too many places in eastern Wyoming to sell stolen goods. Seems like the sheriff's office could have checked those out by now."

"Maybe selling the stuff isn't the point." She was frustrated enough to say exactly what she thought. "Maybe just making us miserable is the goal."

"Which leads us back to the kids."

Jess nodded, but then saw Caroline standing behind Dylan. "I understand why you don't want to believe this is linked to one of the teenagers," she told the other woman. "But they are complicated creatures who don't always return the goodwill they've been offered."

"I know that's true." Caroline slipped past Dylan to enter the room and give Jess a hug. "And if it's one of ours, there will be consequences. Ford called the sheriff's office. Deputy Daughtry will be out tomorrow morning to talk to the kids. We'll try to get some answers as to who's responsible."

"Thanks." Jess tried to let go of her anger, but losing her camera and the photographs was a heavy blow.

She sat down to work with Justino and Lena on their writing after lunch, but found herself more quick-tempered than usual.

Justino's paragraph had been the shortest of all the kids' efforts. He'd written it in Spanish. On the same page, Jess wrote a translation.

I'm not in school and I don't have to finish this stupid writing assignment. When I grow up Lena and I will get married and move to Los Angeles. I will become a famous record producer and make lots of money so I can take care of her the way she deserves. The world I imagine is the one where I'm rich and Lena loves only me.

"Did I get it right?" Jess asked him.

His sullen expression answered without a word.

"I think what you imagine is wonderful. Taking care of people you love is an important goal. I just hoped you would give me some idea of how you planned to do that."

He shrugged. "I said I'd produce records. Latino music," he said emphatically, as if to prove a point.

"How do you get to be a producer?"

"You work for a company. Or you start your own."

"Do you need money to start your own label? Where does that come from?"

Justino surged to his feet, and his chair fell over behind him. "Why the hell are you bugging me about this? I wrote your stupid page. Leave me alone!" He stomped across to the boys' bedroom and slammed the door behind him.

Jess looked at Lena. "Why did he become so upset?"

"He doesn't want to think that it will be hard. Justino likes things to be easy."

"If he doesn't stay in school, that's probably not going to be the case."

The girl sighed. "I know. I try to tell him but he wants the respect of the boys he hangs out with."

"Gang members?"

Lena shrugged and avoided Jess's gaze.

The possibilities for tragedy in this scenario piqued her temper. "Remember the story I told you about my friend Trini? That could so easily be you, Lena, if Justino joins a gang. He won't stay the same sweet guy you love now. And you'll find yourself doing things you never believed you would do, just to keep him." She gripped the girl's arm. "Please, make sure he stays away from that life. For both your sakes."

"Ow." The girl pulled away. "That hurt. We'll be fine. We take care of each other." Her phone, lying on the table, vibrated to signal a message. "Can I go now?"

"Sure."

Jess stacked the papers lying on the table. "That went well." Glancing around the room, she saw Marcos over on the couch, playing a game on his phone. She had meant to talk with him today, too, but after fighting with Justino, it didn't seem like such a good idea. Nate appeared to be deep in his book, and she would hate to disturb him.

Finding Becky meant a walk through the rain to the girls' cabin, but at least she'd be more receptive. Jess wiped her sneakers on the mat outside the door and knocked. "Girls? It's Jess. Can I come in?" She opened the door as she spoke and stepped inside...

…to find Lizzie lying on the couch in a suggestive pose, having her photograph taken by Becky.

With Jess's camera.

"That's mine," Jess said.

"I know. I'm sorry." Becky put the camera in the chair next to where Jess stood. "I'm really sorry."

Lizzie scrambled to sit upright. "We only borrowed it. Really."

"You ask when you borrow something. Taking without asking is stealing."

Both girls hung their heads. Lizzie swiped her fingers over her cheeks.

"Do you have everything else? The computers and the phones?"

Becky looked up in panic. "No. Oh, no. We didn't take anything else. Honest."

"How am I supposed to believe you?"

"Check our stuff. Really, that's the only thing we took." Lizzie rushed to the bedroom and brought back a duffel bag. "See? There's nothing but clothes and makeup."

If only to scare them, Jess pawed through the messy bag. Then she went into the bedroom and made a show of examining the remaining duffels, looking under the beds and in all the closets. She checked the bathroom and the kitchen cabinets, though she'd stopped expecting to find anything.

Back in the living room, she picked up her camera. "I have to report this to Ford and Caroline. I don't have a clue about what they'll decide to do."

"You can't send me home," Lizzie said. "There's nobody there."

"True. But we could hand you over to the sheriff.

He might put you into a foster home under temporary custody until your parents get back." She pretended to consider the idea. "Or into a juvenile detention center. I'm sure there's one in Wyoming somewhere."

Then her despair got the better of her and she gazed at the two of them, sitting side by side on the couch. "I just don't understand why you would risk what you have here. People who care, who are spending money and time on you...for what? An hour's fun? Just because you can? I guess I should know the answer, because I was a kid who made trouble. But mostly I made trouble for myself. I didn't try to hurt other people. Especially not the ones being nice to me."

Jess turned and opened the door. "I guess I'm not as much like you as I thought." Then she crossed the porch and descended the steps, holding the camera under her jacket against the rain.

She found Dylan in his studio, working on the mare and foal sculpture. He looked up as she stepped through the door and she pulled the camera out for him to see.

"You found it? Where?"

"Becky and Lizzie had it."

"What?" He got to his feet. "Did they take everything? Did they do—" he gestured to the rest of the room "—this?"

"No. They invited me to search their bags, and I inspected every cabinet in the house. I believe the camera was separate. Stupid, but separate."

He ran his hands through his hair. "These kids— I hate to say it—but I don't understand how they can stay here. The situation gets worse by the day."

Jess put a hand on his arm. "Wait until tomorrow,

when the deputy comes. If there's new information, or no information, if the kids don't have anything to say…then you can talk to your family about closing the camp." She gave him a wry smile. "As Lizzie pointed out, you're stuck with her till her family returns. I suggested detention or foster care, but those probably aren't real options."

"Too bad," Dylan said, his expression glum. "Maybe we'll just lock her in a stall until her parents can be bothered to show up."

"I'll volunteer for the first shift of guard duty."

That made him laugh. "You would, too." He pulled her into his arms and set his cheek on her hair. "You're a pleasure to have around, Jess Granger. I'm glad you careened into my life last Wednesday afternoon."

"Is that a comment on my driving?"

An argument, especially a manufactured one, was a way to keep her emotions under control. Jess wanted to pull away as easily, as slowly as possible, putting distance between them so the break wouldn't be as hard when it came.

"What do you mean by 'careened'?"

THE SHERIFF'S CAR arrived at promptly 10:00 a.m. on Tuesday morning. Wade Daughtry stepped out, and Dylan could tell he'd taken special care with his uniform to look as official and intimidating as possible. He was a big man, anyway, as tall as Wyatt and square with muscle. Dylan felt a little intimidated himself.

"Hey, Wade." They shook hands and then faced the kids, seated in a line on the edge of the porch. The rain had dried away and the day had dawned bright with sunshine. "Any news?"

"Yes, as a matter of fact. Let me break it all at once."

"It's your show."

Wade nodded to the rest of the Marshall clan and Caroline, and Dylan saw his eyes widen when he caught sight of Jess. But then he got right down to business.

"I'm here because there's been theft and vandalism recently on this property. Phones and computers went missing, along with money and credit cards. Property was damaged, and there was an attempt at arson. I want to ask each of you, at this moment, if you have any information related to these crimes or the person who might have committed these crimes."

Wade stared for a minute at each kid. He started with Becky, who flushed bright red, till all her freckles looked dark brown. She gave a tiny shake of her head. Lizzie, beside her, had gone white. Huddled with her arms wrapped around her waist, she said a silent, "No."

Lena hadn't lost her self-confidence. "Nothing," she said loudly. "I don't know who would do that."

"Turn your phone off," Wade told her, "and put it away till we're done here."

She flashed him a resentful glare, but did as he said.

Justino tried bravado. "You don't have the right to question us," he declared. "We're minors. You need our parents' permission."

"Understand that I'm here for information," Wade said. "If I have to, I'll take you to the office, call your dad and then I'll question you. But you would probably prefer I do it right here." The threat chilled his voice. "Do you know anything about these crimes?"

The boy's "no" sounded small.

Nate didn't have to be asked twice. "I would tell you if I did." But Dylan saw his gaze slide toward Thomas and Marcos, sitting on his other side.

Wade moved to stand directly in front of Thomas and Marcos. "You two have been in trouble before. I'm giving you a chance right now to get out of this before things get rough."

"I don't know nothing," Marcos said.

Thomas snorted. "That's crap. Ask him about his brother Jimmy. Go on, ask him."

Wade looked at Marcos. "Well? Your brother is Jimmy Oxendine. He's got quite a record."

"Maybe, but I didn't have nothing to do with this. Maybe you ought to check *his* friends out." He nodded at Thomas. "Some of them ain't such good guys."

"Don't put this on me." Thomas shoved at Marcos's shoulder. "You're the one who's hanging with a gangsta crew."

The fight exploded in that instant. The boys lunged at each other, all the tensions of the past few days coming to a head. Swearing, punching and kicking, they rolled off the porch and onto the ground as the rest of the kids cleared the area.

Standing closest, Dylan went for Marcos while Wade grappled for a grip on Thomas. Ford and Garrett joined the effort and finally, with one man holding each arm, the four of them pulled the struggling adversaries apart. Bloody noses and swollen eyes testified to the sincerity of their violence.

Before anyone could say a word, a petite dynamo marched into the space between the two. "Enough," Caroline shouted. "That's enough. I'm ashamed of you both." All the fight went out of Thomas and Marcos. They stood slumped and silent.

Dylan did not, however, let go of the arm he held.

"These boys are not going to admit knowing anything," Caroline told Wade. She was as angry with him as with the boys. "If you have news, just tell us. If not, we've got wounds to patch up here."

"We found the phones and computers in a pawn shop down in Cheyenne," Wade said. "And we got a video of the kid who brought them in. Roberto Pena."

Justino jumped to his feet. "I don't believe you. My brother wouldn't do something like this. No way!"

Marcos lifted his head. "I told you I didn't have nothing to do with it."

"So did I." Thomas glared out of a rapidly blackening eye.

"I didn't doubt you," Wade told them. "You're the ones who fought about it."

Now they looked embarrassed as well as battered.

"Why would Roberto come out here to steal?" Justino demanded. "To—to wreck things?"

Ford sent the girls and Nate back to the bunkhouse and the cabin. Now he came to stand beside Justino. "Marcos and Thomas, go to the kitchen with Miss Caroline to get cleaned up and put some ice on those bruises. Justino, we can talk in the living room."

Once they'd settled, Wade explained. "It seems you'd been texting Roberto about this place you were staying and all the nice things just lying around. You know Roberto's been caught stealing before. You know he has a drug habit. Maybe you didn't know how jealous he's been of the deal you've got here."

Justino looked genuinely surprised. "No, I didn't—I wasn't helping him do this. I swear."

Wade glanced at Ford and Wyatt. "I'm leaving that to the Marshalls to decide. But Roberto took advantage of all of you being on the cattle drive, which you told him about, too. And he decided to help himself to some of the property. Then, being the unpredictable sort, he got mad and did some damage. Maybe he thought you'd get blamed, and he'd get even."

Sitting with his head in his hands, Justino started speaking in Spanish. Some of the words even Dylan couldn't translate, but some of them he could. "That's enough."

The boy looked up. "I'll go home. I'm sure you won't want me here anymore. I can only say I'm sorry. I never meant for him—" He shook his head. "He's so messed up."

"We'll talk about it," Wyatt said. "If we have the computers and phones back undamaged, that's the main thing."

"We'll need to keep them for evidence," Wade said. "But eventually they'll be returned to you."

"How old is Roberto?" Ford asked.

"Eighteen," Justino said.

"He'll be tried as an adult," Wade added.

"I'll talk to him." Ford got to his feet. "We'll find out what can be done."

Dylan followed him into the dining room. "Are you saying you're going to offer to defend Roberto on these charges?"

"I'm saying I'll learn what the situation is. He might be able to reduce the sentence if he pleads guilty and gets into rehab."

"Ford, you saw what he did in my studio. He ruined Jess's bag and stole our property. Why would you defend him?"

"Because the legal system works when even the guilty have representation. I'm not the best criminal attorney in the state. But I may be the only one he has access to."

"We have public defenders in this county."

"Overworked, underpaid public defenders. Let it rest for now, Dylan. We'll have a meeting tonight and talk over the options." He went through the door into the kitchen, effectively ending the conversation.

When Dylan turned, he found Jess standing behind him. "Did you hear? Ford—" He broke off, shaking his head. "I can't believe this. That aspect of the man's mind is beyond my comprehension."

"Dylan?" Wade had stepped into the room. "I'm going to head out, unless there's something else you folks need right now."

"No, we've got the facts, finally, thanks to you. When you arrived, I didn't have a chance to introduce you to Jess Granger. Jess, this is Wade. He was a good friend of Ford's in school."

Wade's grin was shy as the two shook hands. "I'd heard Dylan brought a lovely lady into Kate's the other night, but *beautiful* was obviously a better word choice. It's nice to meet you, Jess. I hope you'll be staying around for a while."

"Thanks, Wade. I wish I could stay, but I'll be flying back to New York this week."

Dylan heard the finality in those words. She'd already booked a reservation. Jess had made definite arrangements to leave.

"Well, that's too bad. Maybe you'll visit again sometime soon? Dylan could bring you into town for dinner again."

"It's possible. I can't say I enjoyed this morning, but I do appreciate what you've done."

It's possible in that tone of voice meant *not likely*. And though Dylan had known the inevitable was coming, he still felt as if his insides were being shredded.

"I'll look forward to that," Wade said. He held a hand out. "Take care. If you want my advice, you'll wind up this camp and return those kids to their families. You've got an explosive situation up here."

"I believe I've mentioned that to the people in charge. But the kids deserve help and we're doing what we can."

Wade shook his hand. "Good luck. I'll keep in touch."

"Thanks, buddy." He walked Wade to the front door, and saw Justino still sitting on the couch in the living room. The boy usually carried himself with pride, but at this moment he was hunched over his folded arms, defeated.

Despite his reservations, Dylan couldn't leave him there alone. He sat down on the recliner next to the fireplace. "It'll work out, Justino. If you say you didn't intend for your brother to hurt us, then we'll believe you."

"I'm ashamed that he's done this to your family. And I wish I could make it up to you, what he did to your workshop, your sculptures. But I can't."

"No, you can't. Except by making sure you don't follow his example in your own life. Stay away from the kind of influences that led him to do these things.

That would be what I would ask as a way to make amends."

Justino nodded. "I understand. Can I be excused now?"

"Yes." Dylan figured the boy would make a bee-line for Lena—he hadn't realized she'd been waiting on the front porch until he saw them walking away together, hands tightly clasped.

Jess came into the living room and sat where Justino had been. "You are the most amazing man. What you said to him about making amends was perfect."

"It's the only thing he can do."

"But not everyone would have been able to forgive and forget that way."

Dylan shrugged, feeling his cheeks heat up. "I guess, from what you said to Wade, that you're getting ready to leave. Had enough of the Wild, Wild West this morning? It's been pretty rowdy, I'll say that."

"No. But I have to go back."

"I know." He got to his feet, suddenly very tired. "I just hoped maybe I'd get a chance to change your mind before you left."

Chapter Eleven

The meeting Ford had promised took place late in the evening, after a morning of rodeo practice and another bareback lesson for Lizzie, plus a long trail ride in the afternoon. The overall mood was tense, given the morning's revelations, but Jess enjoyed her tour through different parts of the ranch. She found herself blinking away tears as she brushed out Cash's coat. He'd been a good friend to her.

Over a chili dinner, Caroline told the teenagers they could watch weeknight television that evening, something they hadn't been allowed to do since coming to the ranch. Jess couldn't help being pleased that most of them kept books in the vicinity as they sat around the bunkhouse—even Marcos had laid his baseball book on the arm of the sofa. He wasn't reading it, but the possibility existed, which she considered a real achievement. Although her time with the kids had been short, she liked the idea that she'd made a difference in someone else's life.

With the kids occupied, the Marshall brothers and Caroline took their coffee and pieces of the apple pie Susannah had made into the living room and settled in the various chairs. Jess stayed with Susannah in the kitchen, but the open doorways made the conversation easy to hear.

"So, we have some issues to deal with," Ford said, his voice calm and cool. Jess smiled as she realized she could recognize each brother's voice, having known the four of them for a only week. "We were aware this project would be a challenge when we took it on. I admit, these are the kinds of problems I foresaw when Caroline proposed the plan. But while I opposed the idea to begin with, I now believe we should do everything we can to keep the camp functioning with all the kids here. The question is…how?"

"I agreed with Ford from the outset." Dylan's tone carried more energy, more urgency. "Because I was thinking about this show I have coming up and the work I wanted to complete. I understand that these teenagers need help, that their lives are at a tipping point, for better or for worse. But we're the ones taking the punishment, here. I suggest we at least rearrange the program, make the schedule less intense. Have them on the ranch a couple of times a week, rather than staying here 24/7. I'll drive around and pick them up myself, on the days they come. It would reduce our risk. There's nothing to guarantee the same kind of crazy situation won't come up again."

"The judge handed Justino, Marcos and Thomas over to my custody," Caroline pointed out. "If they aren't here, they go into a community service program five days a week."

"Then they could come here on the weekends," Dylan replied. "Why wouldn't that work?"

"I'm tied up at church all day Sunday," Garrett said. "I wouldn't be here to help. And I think sending them home for most of the week dumps them into the environment we are trying to neutralize in the first place."

"We can't save the world," Dylan countered.

"We can try." Ford and Caroline said it together and there was laughter—though not, Jess thought, from Dylan.

"Wyatt, what about you?" Ford asked.

"We've had trouble, and I regret that." The oldest Marshall's voice was deep and measured. "But I'm of the same opinion now as at the beginning. We owe Henry MacPherson to help other kids the way he helped us."

"So we just continue on with the same plan?" Dylan's patience had worn thin. "Not protecting ourselves, not making any effort to counteract the violence that shows up on an almost daily basis?"

"That's exaggerating, Dylan." Garrett was irritated. "Come down off your high horse."

Jess caught her breath. "He shouldn't have said that," she whispered. Across the counter, Susannah shook her head, apprehension in her wide eyes.

"My high horse? No, actually, that was not one of the sculptures that got damaged when Justino's brother vandalized my studio. Thanks for your concern."

Garrett tried to retreat. "Look, I didn't mean—"

"And don't worry about the destruction of Jess's property, either. Some makeup, a leather bag—no big deal. She gets her phone and computer back, and we'll cover the cash." The rocking chair creaked, as it did when someone stood up. "Except that a guest in our house can't assume she's safe because we've got criminal elements on the property."

"Dylan, sit down." That was Ford.

"No. Because not only did we have a drug addict running rampant when we were out of the way, but two of the girls felt comfortable enough to walk into Jess's room and take her camera. 'Just borrowing,' they said. Right."

"Becky and Lizzie?" Caroline asked, her voice shaky.

"Of course. Because Lena and her boyfriend are always around some corner, making out." That wasn't precisely true...

...and they let him know it. "They've been cooperative."

"We keep a close eye on those two."

"They understand the rules."

"The real problem—" Dylan's voice cut through the protests "—is that you all are willing to take the risks. First, because you care. And that's admirable. But second, I think you've each got some pride involved here in making this project turn out well. You want to be able to say that you saved these kids from disaster."

Heated denials rang through the house.

Dylan spoke over them again. "And third, because you don't care about the damage. Wyatt hardly uses his cell phone. A computer is easy enough to replace. We pay Jess for hers, and she's taken care of. But nobody else has put hundreds of hours into building statues that can be destroyed in the blink of an eye. Thank God, Roberto is a lousy arsonist, or I might have lost almost every piece of work I've done in the last two years. The entire exhibit for the Denver showing is sitting in my studio. Not to mention that studio is my home.

"But for you guys, my art is a hobby. A sideline.

Something I can do to keep me occupied and out of your way. That was the plan when I was a kid, right? 'Here's some paper and crayons, Dylan. Go draw something. We're busy.'"

"You know it's more than that," Wyatt said.

"I do. You don't. You don't understand the *need* I have to create. The burn to shape and mold and carve and bend, to watch meaning come into existence beneath your hands. It's not fun, it's not entertaining or soothing. It's vital."

Jess found herself wiping tears off her cheeks.

"You don't understand that this—making art— is the only connection I have to my past. I can't remember our mother. Not the flicker of an image, not a sound or a smell. I have one sketch from her as my childhood memory. But when I draw, when I build, I am grounded. I'm certain of where I come from.

"Having the kids here threatened me in a way that none of you has experienced. And so you want to go on the same way, with the same possible outcomes. But I can't do it anymore."

His boot heels sounded on the wood floor. Jess headed for the living room.

Caroline and the other Marshall brothers were on their feet. "Where are you going?" Ford asked. "What are you planning to do?"

"Dylan, settle down," Garrett ordered. "We can work this out."

Wyatt cut across them with a single question. "Are you leaving?"

Dylan paused at the door and turned around with a surprised expression on his face. "No, of course not. This is home."

"Then what do you mean when you say you can't do it anymore?"

"The art. I'll stop."

"You can't do that," Jess blurted out. She looked at Wyatt and then Ford. "Don't let him stop."

Dylan's face was surprisingly calm. "It's okay, Jess. I told you—if it came to a choice between family and art, I choose my family."

"But you don't have to choose," she said.

All of the people in the room stared at her. "It's not just about the vandalism," Dylan said. "The time demands, the fragmented attention—I can't keep struggling between the ranch and sculpture."

She stepped next to him and put a hand on his arm. "I know. But what I've come to realize is that the art you make is all about your family. For the last two years, every sculpture you've built has been an aspect of your brothers and the life you share with them. Not just the forms of the creatures you observe here on the ranch, but the spirit you embody as you work, the aspirations you have for the land, the animals and each other.

"Do you think it's a coincidence," she said, gazing straight into his eyes, "that your most recent piece is a mare and foal? That image of nurturing reflects what's going on at the ranch now, as your family works with these kids and strives to help them grow up into strong, healthy adults."

"That makes sense," he said slowly. "What I do in the studio isn't in spite of the family and the ranch. It's my way of expressing what's important to me. Which is the family."

"But you don't have to be a cowboy," Jess said

more softly. "The choices you make and the values you cherish join you to this family."

Dylan shook his head. "The ranch is who we are. It's what we do."

"We're brothers, first and always," Wyatt said. "The ranch came after."

"Long after," Ford agreed. "Henry MacPherson saved us by bringing us here, without a doubt. But that doesn't obstruct our personal choices. I'm an attorney, remember?"

"And I serve a church," Garrett added. "We don't take these careers any less seriously because we're also involved on the Circle M. Even this summer, when Wyatt's out of commission, I'm still preaching, still visiting members."

"And I'm meeting with clients," Ford said. "We all work around each other's commitments. You've been here every day. You know how it goes."

"But you left your San Francisco practice," Dylan said. "You gave it up for the ranch."

"I *chose* to rejoin my family. The same way you did, two years ago." Ford put his arm around Caroline and pulled her close against his side. "I love the land, don't get me wrong. But it's the people that matter."

Hands on his hips, Dylan dropped his chin to his chest. "I get consumed by the process. Walking out of the studio just kills me when I'm so deeply involved." He lifted his head. "That's what I mean. This isn't a hobby, something I can do in my off-hours. I need... more time. All the time there is."

"Maybe we haven't paid enough attention to what you need," Garrett said.

"Could be we didn't take your complaints seriously." Wyatt held his youngest brother's gaze. "That can change."

"Nobody will ever replace you around here," Ford said. "But we can hire somebody to handle most of your jobs."

Dylan let his jaw drop. "You're serious? You'd go that far?"

"You deserve the life you want to live," Wyatt said. "If you can be satisfied here with us while you create the art that drives you, then we'll make it happen."

Garrett came over and put a hand on his shoulder. "And we'll talk with the kids about security. Maybe they can try going without their phones for a day. Or a week. Who knows, maybe we can switch over to using phones only on weekends. We have been naive, as you said. We'll beef up security, change locks, whatever we have to do to make the place more secure. Including your workshop."

"Especially my workshop," Dylan said. "But thanks. I appreciate the thought. And will you take over my morning feedings?"

His brother sighed. "You're going all the way with this, aren't you?"

Dylan laughed. "Man, you'd better believe it."

WHEN THE MEETING finally ended, Dylan took Jess back to the studio. With the lights on, he walked around the place, taking a fresh view of his own work.

"You're right," he told her, still surprised. "I couldn't see the forest for the trees, so to speak. But it's here. All of us, our personalities, we're here. The buffalo—that's Wyatt. The fox is Garrett and Ford is the eagle. I'm the elk. And I don't know if you've noticed this one…" He went to a spot near the end of a table, and picked up a small figure. "These are rock wrens, nesting. Reminds me of Caroline."

"That's very sweet. I hadn't noticed it before." She came to take the statue from him. "You're right— that's Caroline taking care of everybody."

"But I believe I'll have to create a new piece for you. An owl—a western screech owl."

Her frown appeared on the instant. "I don't screech!"

He tilted his head. "Can you say that a little louder?" She pouted at him when he grinned. "But you are wise, like the owl. You've made such a difference in my life." Taking her hands, he pulled her to stand in front of him. "And now you're going away. Is there anything I can say to change your mind?"

From the regret on her face, Dylan guessed the answer. "Then I won't try. We'll just enjoy the rest of our night. Come upstairs with me."

He feared she might say she had to pack, or get some sleep. But Jess simply smiled and led the way. "It will be my pleasure," she said quietly.

When he woke up in the morning, she was gone.

But lying on top of the covers were the two sketches he'd done—the bust of Wyatt and his version of his mother's drawing. Jess must have pulled them out of the trash. She hadn't left a note, but he got the message.

Do these, she might as well have said. *It's time.*

Dylan worked through the rest of the summer, hour upon hour of focused effort he'd never before enjoyed. When he was stuck, he'd take a ride on Leo, or help the kids with their rodeo lessons, but he could walk away now, return to his studio and concentrate anew. He slept at night, his bed comfortable, if lonely. Jess's absence was a constant ache, like a stitch in his side every time he moved. The only solace was his work.

As the fall started, he found himself spending longer hours, staying up later and feeling almost as tired as if he were still doing ranch chores. The kids went back to school and the ranch quieted down. Wyatt began picking up more of the ranch responsibilities—which was a relief to everybody because he'd become increasingly grumpy about "sitting around doing nothing."

October brought the issue of *Renown Magazine* with his article in it. Kip ordered a hundred copies and managed to hang on to two—one for Wyatt, Ford and Garrett and one for Dylan. But he had already received his own copy in the mail from Jess—the first he'd heard from her since the summer. He'd thought about calling, emailing, even writing a letter…but he didn't intend to stalk her. They'd had a summer affair, and now it was over. If he was still in love, that was just too bad for him.

The article was beautifully written, of course, and made him sound downright glamorous.

"Working in a secluded woodland setting, with Crazy Woman Creek running nearby, Dylan Marshall crafts his sculptures one meticulous piece at a time, assembling the whole image with the patience of a Zen master. Having renovated a working barn for his edgy and yet entirely functional studio, Marshall collects his materials from the landscape around him, a new approach to the concept of 'found art.' Although

not abstract in the traditional sense, the figures
emerge from his construction process in spiritual form, representative of concepts and para-
digms only hinted at by his earlier nonfigurative
work..."

Dylan laughed as he read the ten-dollar words, so
typical of the overblown prose he'd once been used
to hearing in the art world. "Doesn't mean a damn
thing," he said to himself. "Except that she likes the
way it looks." The article skirted the whole issue about
why he'd abandoned the art world—"a personal crisis
of confidence," Jess had called it, "a reassessment of
his work and its place in the world." He wondered if
that had been specific enough to save her job.

She'd scrawled across the front cover of the magazine, "You're famous... Again! Love, Jess." He wished
she meant that the way he would.

November arrived. He and his brothers spent days
building custom crates for each of the sculptures,
packing and padding them and moving them into a
horse trailer for transportation to the gallery. He made
the drive down to Denver by himself the week before, but his family would be arriving on the day of
the show, as would Patricia Trevor, the gallery owner.
Fortunately, the manager and the security guard at the
gallery helped him unload and arrange the exhibit. It
wasn't the premium treatment he'd received when the
art world thought he was on fire.

But Dylan knew where this work had come from
and what it meant, which was what mattered to him
now. And the exhibit was beautiful—the gallery pro-
vided linen-covered blocks of different heights for the

sculptures, with linen screens dividing the large space into more intimate rooms and giving the pieces the right scale. Track lighting on the ceiling ensured that beams of light illuminated the colors and grains of the woods he'd used, making every figure seem to glow on its own. The walls of the gallery itself were plate glass windows looking out on the city, adding a sense of motion and energy. Dylan couldn't have asked for a more perfect setting in which to show off his art.

On the day of the show, he went to his hotel in the late afternoon to shower and change. After so many weeks of hard work, he allowed himself to lie down for just a few minutes to rest his burning eyes and aching back.

The ringing phone woke him up. "Where the hell are you?" Ford said. "The crowd's here and the artist isn't. What's going on?"

"Ten minutes," Dylan yelled into the phone as he dragged off his jeans. "Ten minutes!"

He arrived at his first show in almost three years with his hair still damp and the aroma of shaving cream lingering around his face. Garrett opened the door as he reached it. "Late, as usual," he said, leaning in for a one-armed hug. "Go get 'em."

Dylan could barely make his way across the room for the crowd. Patricia had hoped for an attendance of twenty, but this seemed to be closer to two hundred. He wasn't sure how to find her in the press of people, but then a tiny, white-haired woman with bloodred fingernails latched on to his arm.

"Just like the old days," she said, in the haughty tones he recognized from their two phone conversations. "Always assuming the attention will be there when you deign to appear." Then she raised her voice. "Ladies and gentlemen, please let me introduce you to my newest protégé—renowned artist and sculptor Dylan Marshall."

After that, he couldn't see farther than three feet in front of him because there was always someone standing right there, shaking his hand, admiring his work, offering to pay three or four times whatever he asked for one of his statues. He probably seemed to be the arrogant artiste to them...or else really stupid. He just couldn't think of what to stay, couldn't take everything in. In his wildest dreams, he'd never expected—

Jess.

As one person in front of him moved out of the way, he saw her. She stood all the way on the other side of the room, champagne glass in hand, wearing a short skirt and tall heels. And staring straight at him.

Dylan started walking, brushing past people who spoke to him, sidestepping those who tried to block his progress. Jess moved toward him, and people stepped out of her way, until they were confronting each other across the centerpiece of the show—the mother and child sculpture he'd built through the summer and the fall.

"I didn't realize you were coming," was his brilliant opening line.

"I couldn't stay away." She frowned at him. "You're thin. You haven't been eating."

"I've been working, though."

She nodded. "I can see that. It's...breathtaking. More beautiful than I could possibly have imagined."

"So are you." Dylan glanced around at the crowd,

wishing for a moment of privacy. "When did you get into Denver?"

"Later than I intended."

"How long are you staying?"

"As a matter of fact—"

At that moment, Patricia sank her claws into him again. "Come with me. The mayor wants to talk to you about a commission."

"But—" He looked over his shoulder, flung out a hand...

...and felt Jess's palm against his. "I'm here," she said, when he drew her close. "I'll be right here."

With Jess's hand in his, the rest of the evening passed easily. She had her own fans in the crowd, people who had read the *Renown* article on Dylan and had come because of it, as well as people who read the magazine because of Jess Granger's writing.

There were conversations about abstract versus representational art, carving versus mosaic, different woods and glues and stains—Dylan maintained his focus through them all, remembering names and faces, accepting compliments and the occasional criticism with assurance. He didn't require anyone else's good opinion. His brothers were here. Jess stood by his side. His world was complete.

The chaos began to subside about 9:00 p.m. "We have dinner reservations," Garrett said as his brothers prepared to return to their hotel. "We'll wait for you at the restaurant."

"Right..." He'd lost Jess for a moment in the bustle, but then found her in a corner, engaged in serious conversation with a man whose face people across the country had seen many times on their television and theater screens. Waving goodbye to the stragglers just leaving, Dylan made his way over and stood nearby, trying not so subtly to eavesdrop.

But they'd finished their talk. "I'll be in touch," the actor told Jess, and gave her his card. Then he shook Dylan's hand. "Great exhibit. I bought two of the pieces—love that screech owl and the mare and foal. I've got just the places for them in my new house." In an instant, he slipped out the door and into a limousine waiting at the curb.

Dylan looked at Jess. "Was that really—"

She nodded. "He offered me a job. As the editor of a new magazine."

"But...you have a job."

"Um, no. I resigned."

He cleared his throat. "Why?"

"I realized I wanted to do something more than entertain, or even inform. Working with the kids...even for just a few days...that changed me. I want—I *need* to do something that makes a difference in people's lives. Maybe even grumpy teenagers' lives."

"Do you know what that is?"

Jess smiled. "I'm not sure. Teaching, maybe?"

Dylan took her hands in both of his and raised them to his lips. "You would be an amazing teacher."

Around them, the gallery was closing down, the lights shutting off. Having locked the door, the manager began pulling shades over the glass windows. "Gotta go, Dylan," he called. "I want some dinner."

"Right." Looking around, Dylan surveyed the collection of his work, some of which he wouldn't ever see again. "An amazing night," he said. Then he turned to Jess. "Mostly because you were here. Why did you come?"

Without waiting for an answer, he led her through the back room of the gallery and out into the alley, and then around to the sidewalk. Snow had started to fall.

"Perfect," he said, still holding her hand. "We haven't had any snow at home yet." Realizing he was stalling, he faced her. "Now, tell me. Why are you here?"

Snowflakes perched on her long hair and on her eyelashes. "I expected to go back to my life. Write the article and move on. I mean, I knew I wouldn't stop loving you, but I could live with it. I thought."

Dylan blinked at her. "You didn't say you loved me. Before."

"I was trying to do the right thing. Offering you a chance to find somebody who would give you kids. Making it easier by not telling you I love you, too." Her gloved hands covered her face. "I was so stupid."

"Yes."

She let her hands fall away and laughed. "Instead, it's only gotten worse. Like freezing to death—I'm a little colder every day when I'm not with you. Eventually, I'll just fall asleep and die. Emotionally, anyway. And what good will I be to myself or anyone else if I freeze over?"

He took hold of her shoulders. "What do you want, Jess?"

"I want to be alive, Dylan, the way you are. You and your brothers and Caroline and Susannah—you don't just exist, as I've just existed my whole life. You *live*. And I want to live, too. I can't give you your own children. But I'll give you everything I have."

Anger flooded through him. "Do you realize how miserable I've been?"

Jess nodded. "I do. I've been miserable myself."

"You wasted months when we could have been happy together."

"I know. I'm sorry."

"And now you want to just waltz back and take up where we left off? I suppose you want a proposal, too. A wedding and all that goes with it?"

She swallowed hard. "Yes, please."

He glared at her, frozen by wrath…and then in an instant it melted away like spring frost. "Okay. Now come here."

Wrapping her in his arms, he brought their mouths together and erased the past five months with kisses, hot and seeking and wild, completely inappropriate for a city sidewalk and completely necessary as he reclaimed the love he thought he'd never hold again.

"Get a room, why don't you," yelled somebody walking past them.

Dylan drew back. "I have a room. How long do you suppose my brothers are prepared to wait?"

Jess grinned. "Would all night be too long?"

"Not for me," Dylan told her. "Forever isn't long enough for me."

* * * * *

5_ST19

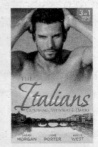

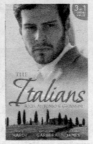

MILLS & BOON®

Why shop at millsandboon.co.uk?

Each year, thousands of romance readers find their perfect read at millsandboon.co.uk. That's because we're passionate about bringing you the very best romantic fiction. Here are some of the advantages of shopping at www.millsandboon.co.uk:

* **Get new books first**—you'll be able to buy your favourite books one month before they hit the shops

* **Get exclusive discounts**—you'll also be able to buy our specially created monthly collections, with up to 50% off the RRP

* **Find your favourite authors**—latest news, interviews and new releases for all your favourite authors and series on our website, plus ideas for what to try next

* **Join in**—once you've bought your favourite books, don't forget to register with us to rate, review and join in the discussions

Visit **www.millsandboon.co.uk**
for all this and more today!